UNTIL THE LAST SPIKE

The Journal of Sean Sullivan

A Transcontinental Railroad Worker

★ WILLIAM DURBIN ★

SCHOLASTIC INC.

Copyright © 1999 by William Durbin

★ ★ ★

ISBN 978-0-545-53080-4

★ ★ ★

12 11 10 9 8 7 6 5 4 3 2 1   13 14 15 16 17 18/0

Printed in the U.S.A.   40
This edition first printing, September 2013

The display type was set in Wells Grotesque Medium.
The text type was set in Berling.
Book design by Steve Scott
This edition photo research by Amla Sanghvi

To Barbara Markowitz,
agent, advocate, and friend

And to my granddaughters,
Olive and Abigail, with love

Omaha, Nebraska
1867

August 6, 1867
Omaha, Nebraska

I saw my first scalp today and I have to admit that it scared me good. I arrived at the train depot in Omaha, scheduled to meet my pa. His train was a few minutes late, so I walked around the station, studying all the activity. Peddlers were hawking everything from fruit and motion-sickness pills to accident insurance and real estate. INVEST IN THE WEST, one sign read, and under it sat a man with slicked-back hair, who was selling stock in a silver mine.

When the big Union Pacific steam engine finally chugged up to the platform, I walked over to greet Pa. I figured it wouldn't be hard to find him, since he was riding in on a freight like workmen sometimes do. The first man to get off the train was a pale fellow with a bloody bandage wrapped around his head. His neck and right arm were also bandaged with strips of red-stained cloth. He was carrying a water pail in his left hand. When a lady behind me let out a squeal, a crowd immediately gathered.

"Excuse me," the conductor said, stepping forward to help the man get through the curiosity seekers, "there's been an accident." As the pale man passed by, I glanced down into his bucket and saw what looked like a drowned muskrat without a tail.

I was staring openmouthed when Pa walked up beside me and touched my shoulder. "I'm sorry you had to see that, Sean," he said. Normally there is no missing my pa in a crowd—he's six foot three and has lively green eyes that get your attention from a long way off—but I was so rattled that I never even saw him until he spoke.

"Was that a—?"

"A scalp." Pa nodded. He said he hoped that the Indian trouble would be over by now, but that there had been a little flare-up lately. Pa stopped and stared at me. "Are you all right, Sean? I hope it wasn't a mistake to bring you out here."

I swallowed deeply and shook my head. "I'm fine," I lied. For a whole year, I'd been begging to join Pa in his work on the Transcontinental Railroad. I wanted him to know I was grown up enough to handle this.

"That poor Englishman." Pa shook his head. He explained that the man's name was Bill Thompson. Last night, he'd gone out with a crew of five men to check a dead telegraph line, but it was a trap. Their handcar hit a tie that the Cheyennes had laid across the tracks. The men and all their tools flew into the air. They never had a chance. The Indians shot and scalped everyone. Only minutes later the crew of a night freight steamed into that same barricade. The train crashed, impaling engineer Bully Bowers on the throttle lever and pitching his fireman face first against the firebox, where he roasted to death. Meanwhile, Thompson, who had lain still and pretended he was dead, saw that his scalp had dropped off a brave's belt. He picked it up and started back toward the Plum Creek station, where he was rescued by a troop train.

"Where's he headed now?" I asked, stunned that anyone could be that tough.

"He hopes the doc here in Omaha can patch him back up."

August 7, End of Track
West of Lodgepole Creek, Nebraska

Yesterday passed in a dizzying rush. I still can't believe I'm here. Our train passed through a string of railroad towns that everyone back in Chicago is always talking about: Elkhorn, Fremont, Columbus, and Grand Island.

There isn't much to the prairie—it's just big patches of dry yellow grass stretching as far as you can see. Pa says there's millions of wildflowers in the spring, but it's hard to believe.

Just west of a place called Kearney, we saw a dozen covered wagons. Pa pointed and said, "That's what's left of the Oregon Trail." I see why they call them "prairie schooners." With their big canvas tops puffed out in the breeze, they looked like they were sailing over the grass.

Near Elm Creek, I saw my first buffalo herd. The shaggy-haired animals were more than a quarter of a mile away, but I could tell they were enormous. The next thing I knew, someone fired a rifle right behind me, and I nearly jumped out of my skin. I turned to see a half-dozen rifles pointed out the train windows and shooting away. The noise was awful, but the buffalo, who were well out of rifle range, kept meandering along. When the gunfire stopped, a man near the back of the car shouted, "I got one," and another said, "So did I."

"They never came close," Pa sneered. "We call them 'excursionists.'" Though Pa is normally not much of a talker, I could tell he was proud to teach me about the West. "They are itching to go back East and brag that they shot a buffalo," he said, "but the cowcatchers — we call them 'pilots' out here — on the front of our trains kill more buffalo than all these silly fools added together."

Just before we got to the Plum Creek station, the passengers checked their six-shooters and rifles and made sure they had extra ammunition in case of an Indian attack.

I must have looked nervous, because Pa told me not to worry. "Plum Creek is filled with soldiers right now," he said. "The redskins ain't about to take your hair here." I was about to say something about him calling the Indians "redskins"—Mother had never allowed him to use that word—but I decided it wouldn't be right to start an argument on our first day together.

Though Mother's been dead for three years, I can remember how she'd chew him out whenever he spoke badly of the Indians. "Patrick Sullivan," she'd say, "those natives have been here a lot longer than you Irish."

And when Pa would remind her that she was Irish, too, she'd toss her red hair back and say, "It's not my better half."

I knew she was teasing him then, because though she was part German, she was just as proud of being Irish as Pa is.

Another reason I let Pa's remark pass was that I wanted to see what things were really like out West. Maybe working on the prairie and seeing what happened to men like Bill Thompson could turn anyone against the Indians.

We had a short stop in North Platte, the final destination for everyone who wasn't going on to Ogallala or Julesburg. Since the Oregon Trail crosses the river here and swings north, there were quite a few covered wagons in town. Pa said it was foolish of the settlers not to wait for the Union Pacific to finish the railroad. "They could cover in a day what they'll make in a whole summer in those wagons," he said.

After we ate at a little hotel, Pa showed me the town. "There's the Platte River," he said. "People joke that it's a foot deep and a mile wide."

That looked pretty close to the truth to me. The Platte was just a big mudflat with a trickle of brown water headed no place in particular and crossed by a shaky-looking trestle. Beside the tracks was a big, ten-stall brick roundhouse, a wood-frame depot, and a hotel. The other buildings on Main Street looked new but empty. I asked Pa what was wrong.

He kicked at a dry stalk of yellow weed and said, "North Platte's dying fast. This place had three thousand people in it last spring and now it's down to one hundred fifty." He explained that the railroad was the only reason the prairie towns came to be, and when the road builders moved on, the money moved with them. He said that people are always tagging along with the road, "hoping to make a fast buck, or chasing a dream." And whether it's gold or silver or good land they're after, they all keep heading West.

When I asked where all the people had gone, he waved his hand to the west and said, "Most of them are just up the line in Julesburg. But there's lots of fellows over there who never had a chance to move on."

Pa pointed to an unfenced cemetery. The irregular rows of wooden grave markers were tilted at wild angles.

I asked him if a big storm had tipped the markers.

"We see plenty of wind out here," he said, "but that's not the problem. The earth settles real fast over a fresh-dug grave, and there's nobody left in this town to care."

August 8

I just woke up and have a world of things to tell. Since we got in late last night, I didn't have a chance to mention the biggest surprise of all. It happened in Julesburg, a place known as a "hell-on-wheels" town because the U.P. workers go there to blow off steam. As we pulled into the station to take on wood and water, Pa told me that the town was so wild that they averaged a killing every single day.

I figured he had to be stretching things, so while he was chatting with a conductor friend of his, I took a walk. Since it was late in the day, piano playing and loud talking were already coming from the saloons. A lady in a shiny black dress walked by. She was wearing the tallest hat I'd ever seen. It was made of green silk and white feathers and swayed from side to side when she walked. There are lots of fancy women back in Chicago, but I'd never seen one dangling a silver derringer from her pocket chain. She smiled at me and said, "Hey there, Junior." I lowered my eyes and walked on real fast.

I crossed over to the far side of the street and hustled back toward the depot. That's when I saw a pair of boots sticking out from behind a building. I peeked around the corner and nearly jumped out of my skin. A dead man was lying flat on his back with his eyes fixed straight up at heaven.

I sucked in a quick breath and took off running. Though I was gone in the tick of a second hand, the picture of that man froze in my mind: the blank stare, the dried-blood patch on his shirt, the cigar stub on the ground still giving off a tiny wisp of smoke. But the thing that told the most was the man's pockets: Every single one was turned inside out.

When I got back to the train, I was busting to tell Pa what I'd seen, but the moment I saw him, I remembered what he'd said back in Omaha about it being a mistake to bring me out West. So all I could do was swallow my words and try to calm the pounding of my heart.

Evening

Though I start work tomorrow, I've promised myself to make time to write in this journal as often as I can. I owe that to my mother and, as I found out shortly after she died, I owe it to myself, too. The journal was my mother's idea. The Christmas before she died, when I was twelve, she gave me a blank notebook. On the top of the first page she wrote a quote from a fellow named Sir Francis Bacon: "Reading maketh a full man; conference a ready man; and writing an exact man." The quote made sense to me, but I had to smile when I saw that name. It would be bad enough being called "Francis," but having a last name like "Bacon" would make it a hundred times worse. Can you imagine all the teasing he had to put up with when he was young?

Mother was a teacher but had to quit when she married my pa, because her school only hired single ladies. She missed teaching a lot and kept in practice by helping me and my brother, John — he's two years younger than me — with our schoolwork and sharing stories and quotes from her favorite writers. John and I both got tired of studying at times, but before we got bored, she'd switch to something lively like Robin Hood or Finn MacCool or King Arthur. We could never get enough of her tales about Arthur's magician, Merlin.

Mother also copied some lines from a poem that I didn't understand. It went something like, "What oft was thought but ne'er so well expressed." Mother loved fancy language like that. She explained the lines of that poem by saying, "Lots of people claim to think great things, but it's a rare man who has the discipline to write them down."

Though she said those words nearly four years ago, I've never forgotten them. And I've learned firsthand that writing can help a person. After Mother died, I put my journal away and I didn't write in it for two or three months. Then one day for no reason I started writing about how I was so angry at her for dying that I was never going to write again. But after I'd scrawled out a page filled with questions like why did this have to happen to me? and why would God take away a good woman who was only trying to have a baby? I suddenly realized that writing could help me sort out my sadness.

Now I write all the time. Putting my thoughts down on paper helps me understand what I'm feeling. That might sound strange, but sometimes I'll pick up my pencil because I'm hot mad at someone like my aunt Katie. Yet before I've written down even half of what I aimed to, my anger seems to dry up.

By rights, I shouldn't ever be mad at Katie. She and Uncle Willy were the ones who looked after me and my brother back in Chicago after my mother died. It happened so sudden that me and John would have been in a bad way if they hadn't helped out. Pa was off in the war when Mother had her trouble. She was grinnin' and jokin' one day, then the next thing you know she and her newborn baby were dead. With Pa gone, I hate to think what would have happened to us if we hadn't had Katie and Willy.

We wrote to my pa three or four times, but he was marching with a general named Sherman, and our letters didn't catch up with him until two months had passed. When Pa finally came home, he was lost in his sadness for a long time. I think he felt guilty because Mother had been having trouble with babies for a long time. "I shoulda been here," he'd said, and no matter how much Katie and Willy tried to convince him that the war had left him no choice, he'd just shake his head and say, "I woulda run off if I'd knowed."

At times, I'd find Pa staring off into blank space. I'd talk straight at him, but it was like I wasn't there. Once when he was standing by the parlor window in the dark, I even heard him whispering to himself.

After a while, Pa went back to work on the railroad—he'd hired on with the Chicago and Alton line before the war—and when General Jack Casement came through town and offered to hire him on as a foreman for the Union Pacific, he declined at first. But my aunt encouraged him to sign on. She promised to take good care of us and said that working on the Transcontinental Railroad was a duty as important as the war had been.

I was mad at Aunt Katie for convincing him to go, and even when she explained why it was important for Pa, I only half understood. "Your pa needs to find a part of himself that he lost in the war," she said. "The West may be the answer."

Now when I see my pa out here, laughing and talking again, I know she was right.

I can already tell that working on this railroad isn't always going to be simple, but this journal should help me think things through. Sometimes Pa used to say that a man could accomplish a heck of a lot more with a shovel than a pen, but Mother wouldn't let him get away with it. "Patrick Charles Sullivan," she'd say, putting her hands on her hips and looking him straight in the eye even though she had to tilt her head way back since my pa is so tall, "I don't want a son who's all brawn and no brains. We are entering the age of the machine, and a man's mind is going to get him a blamed sight further than his muscles."

August 9

When Pa told me that I'd have to start at the bottom, he wasn't kidding. My job is water carrier. Pa is proud to be a Union Pacific foreman, and he doesn't want anyone to think I'm getting special treatment because I'm his son. Since I'm already fifteen, I had hoped I could do more than boy's work.

Pa introduced me to Jack Casement, the contractor for all of the Union Pacific Railroad's tracklaying. Though Pa figures Mr. Casement is only five feet four inches—that's six inches shorter than me—he looks a lot taller. Maybe it's the stiff and upright way he carries himself that gives him extra size. He's got a wild, bushy beard, and dark eyes that pierce right through you. A big-handled six-shooter sticks out of his belt, and he wears black riding boots with mean-looking spurs. Since Mr. Casement was a general during the war, many of the men still call him "General." My pa tells me that he's tough driving but fair.

When I looked at the long bullwhip that he was carrying in his hand, I believed the first, but I guessed I'd have to wait and see about the second.

August 10

I'm too tuckered out to write. Luckily it's Sunday tomorrow, and we get the day off.

★ ★ ★

August 11

I'm getting tired of Pa reminding me to work my hardest. Last night, he must have told me for the one thousandth time, "Everything I got in this life I earned by the sweat of my brow, and you can do the same."

Pa comes from a long line of what he calls "pick-and-shovel" men. His own father died in an accident while digging the Erie Canal, and as a young man, Pa earned his keep working as a "bog trotter" on the Chicago waterfront. He's fond of saying, "People who stroll down Michigan Avenue and look in those fancy shopwindows shouldn't forget that street was a mosquito-infested swamp until we Irishmen carted in six feet of solid fill."

Most of Chicago was built up from a marsh. In my section of town, wooden planks and steps were everywhere because some people had raised their houses up to the six-foot level of the main street and others had only raised theirs partway or not at all. So the boardwalks were pitched at crazy angles, and my uncle Willy, who has a fondness for the bottle, often said, "Chicago's a nightmare for a tippler."

After only two days on the job, I've discovered that being a water carrier is bad for two reasons: 1. Water buckets are very heavy. 2. Men develop a powerful thirst in this dry country.

August 13

I swear my arms have stretched two inches. I'm finally getting used to lugging the water buckets around, but the first couple of days my muscles ached so bad that I could barely lift my hands above my waist.

I have discovered one good thing about my job! I get to see every part of the U.P.'s rail-laying operation. Ben Wharton, the wagon driver, and I deliver water to all of the men working within five miles. At least once a day we take the wagon out to the grading crew—they're the fellows who level the roadbed for the ties. It's so flat around here that it's easy for them to stay ahead of the tracklayers, but Ben says that once we reach the mountains, there'll be enough digging and blasting to keep an army busy. He said that there are already hundreds of men out way ahead of us, working on some tunnels that will take two or even three years to bore all the way through.

The favorite part of my day is bringing water to the spikers. They are a special crew I really admire. Lots of them can pound a spike down in only three swings. They use special hammers with tapered heads called "spike mauls," and their rhythm stays the same all day long. Each time they go after a spike, the steel of their maul rings out clear twice, and then there's a final, flatter *ping* as the spike catches the rail and bites down hard into the wood. Someday I want to drive spikes like that.

August 14

Another thing I like about my job is Ben. Some of the men who were in the Union army during the war call him "Reb" or "Confederate" 'cause he fought with the South. Ben said he was just a cook for his regiment until the commander saw what a good shot he was with a squirrel gun and moved him right up to the front lines. Other fellows say Ben is a "mudsiller."

When I asked Ben if they called him a "mudsiller" because he was a Negro, he threw back his head and laughed. "No, that ain't it at all," he said. "We was so poor back home that our cabin had a puncheon floor and a packed-dirt sill under the door to keep out the wind and rain."

My family never had much money back in Chicago, but at least we had solid wood floors.

Ben has only one good arm, but he works harder than anyone I've ever seen—harder even than my pa. Ben's right arm was shot off at the elbow in the Battle of Droop Mountain, so he's learned to do everything with his left hand. He can drive a mule or a horse team like no one else. Most of the mule skinners use their whips a lot, but Ben talks to his animals instead. "Morning, Flossie," he'll say to his favorite mule, and her ears will perk up like someone had just offered her a peck of sweet apples. And toward the end of the day, when the animals are plumb worn out, he'll just whistle and say, "Ain't much farther to the barn, Honey Chile." And lo and behold, though there isn't a barn within twenty-five miles, those animals will trot double time all the way back to the work train.

August 16

I am amazed at the number of men working on this railroad. The center of activity is General Casement's work train. It is like a small city on wheels. The front cars are loaded with tracklaying materials: switches, timbers, steel rods, lining bars, wrenches, barrels, iron plates, cables, etc. The next car contains a complete feed store and a saddle shop. The third one is a carpenter shop and washhouse. The fourth holds sleeping quarters for the mule skinners, the men who drive the teams. Next in line is a sleeping car that holds 144 bunks. The sixth and seventh are dining halls — the larger one can feed two hundred men at once! Right after that comes a combination kitchen car and telegraph office, followed by a store and eight more sleeping cars. A supply car and two water cars pull up the rear. Five hundred head of beef trail along beside the train to keep us supplied with meat.

One thing that makes me nervous is all the guns. The ceiling of every bunk car is lined with rifles—Pa says there's a thousand of them loaded and ready to go. With all these former Union soldiers just waiting for a chance to use them, how can the Indians be a threat?

August 17

Last night I found out why the Indians are still so dangerous. It happened just as we were getting ready to bunk out for the night. Pa prefers sleeping in a tent in the hot weather, and I'm glad because those bunk cars smell worse than a pig farm. Lots of guys with stronger stomachs than me complain about the stink, and the bedbugs are awful, too. The fellows will do just about anything to avoid the bunk cars. Some have pitched tents on top of the roofs, and a few guys are even sleeping in hammocks they've slung under the flatcars.

Pa and his buddy Bill Flanagan were playing cribbage like they usually do before they go to bed when a bullet whizzed through the side of our tent. I didn't even realize what had happened until a shaving mug exploded on a shelf just above my head. Then a fraction of a second later we heard the report of a rifle, followed by a far-off war whoop. We dove for the floor, but I know it would have been too late if the bullet had been a foot lower.

Pa crawled over to make sure I wasn't hurt and handed me a rifle. Then he tossed Bill his Colt, and we hunkered down tight, waiting for another shot. But the night was dead calm. Someone hollered to see if we were all right, and a few minutes later Pa and Bill slipped outside. Pa's last words were, "If anyone touches that tent flap without whistling first, you let 'em have it."

I kept the Winchester leveled at the door, with my thumb on the hammer, ready to cock it at a moment's notice. I sat in the dark — Pa had blown out the lamp — waiting for a volley of shots, but I only heard a lone coyote calling in the distance.

What seemed like a long time later, Pa whistled and called, "You okay, Sean?"

When I answered back, he stuck his head into the tent. "Not a sign of a livin' soul out there," he said. "They must've lit out for the next county." Then he added with a grin, "Just remember, you don't have to worry about the bullets you can hear."

Bill laughed and said, "Ain't that the truth."

Pa and Bill crawled into bed without even bothering to pick up the broken pieces of that mug. They started snoring right away, but I lay awake for a long time after.

The moon was bright on the prairie, and the shadows of bats and bugs were flickering across the canvas above my head. I couldn't help but wonder how awful it would be to take a stray bullet in the brain and never know why.

August 18

I got a close look at my first Platte River Valley storm this afternoon. Pa had warned me how quick they can blow up, but it was hard for me to believe that it ever rained in this dusty country. It was near quitting time, and Ben and I were heading back to the work train in an empty wagon. It had been hot like usual, but the air was more humid, and the sky had an eerie yellow tint to it. I heard a far-off rumble of thunder, and some puffy, kettle-shaped clouds started swirling in the west. Ben looked over his shoulder and urged his team to hurry. Though we were within sight of the train, I knew we were in trouble.

Just then a jagged trail of lightning flashed across the sky, followed by a big crashing clap of thunder. A gust of wind lifted up the left side of the wagon and nearly flipped us over. Ben threw on the brake and hollered, "We best take cover."

The whole world went black as a wall of rain hit us head-on. We crawled under the wagon, but water poured through the slats in the bed and soaked us through. The wind picked up a notch, and I heard a terrible crashing up ahead. In the next lightning flash, I saw a wagon, framed like a picture between the legs of those mules, splintering to pieces as it rolled over and over.

The storm stopped as quick as it started. I could've kissed Ben's mules for hunkering down and holding their ground. If they'd bolted, we would have come out a lot worse than drenched and muddied up.

I miss my brother, John, more than I ever thought I would. I wrote him a letter tonight, and printing out my return address — Sean Sullivan, End of Track, Union Pacific Railroad — made me more lonesome than ever.

Dear John,

As anxious as I was to see the West, I have found it to be hard country. I used to complain about hauling firewood back home, but that's nothing compared to what they have me doing out here. From dawn to dark, I'm carrying water buckets to the work crews. The fellow I work with is nice enough, but all the other men do is holler, "Bring that dipper here, boy." And no matter how quick I get there, they complain. "This water tastes like pond scum," a fellow told me yesterday. I felt like telling him to get his own drinks, but I thought the better of it.

I miss the sight of blue water. Out here on the prairie, the streams and rivers are all muddy. Even the sky isn't the same sort of blue that I'm used to. With the wagon teams and grading crews kicking up dust all day long, the air is always filled with a dull haze.

Are the apples getting ripe over at Clarkson's orchard? I sure am hungry for a piece of Aunt Katie's pie. I'd give a week's pay just to sit down to a meal of her fried chicken.

Your brother,
Sean

August 19

I never get tired of watching the tracklayers work. There's a rhythm to the operation that makes it look graceful, almost like a dance. The "joint-tie men" are out ahead of everyone. Working in twos, they bed a tie every fourteen feet. "Fillers" then set the rest of the ties for the eight "iron men," who slide out the 560-pound rails and, at the command of "down," drop them into place. Next come the "spikers," who gauge the width of the rails and pound down the spikes. Once the fishplates are bolted tight at the rail seams, the "track liners" use crowbars to adjust the final alignment of the rails.

As the spikers are driving their last spikes, "back iron men" are pulling the next load of rails forward on a horse cart. As soon as the rails are slid off the rollers, they dump the empty cart to the side and hustle back to reload. It all starts just past sunup and goes on all day—the rails thunk down, the spike mauls *ping* on steel, and the dusty wheels of the supply wagons creak up and down the right-of-way.

When the rails are going down, I've got to be close at hand with my water pail and tin dipper, especially during the heat of the day. If the fellows want a drink, they'll yell if I'm not Johnny-on-the-spot.

The orneriest fellow I've met so far is a big man named Mac O'Grady. If I'm more than two steps away, he'll growl, "Is that damned water boy napping again?" Then he laughs if I trip on a rail because I'm hurrying so much.

The men are meanest on Mondays because they're still feeling the effects of their weekend whiskey. It's a wonder that the fellows don't get sick from the water. By the time we haul it from the main tank at the rear of the train, it's a little muddy, and after a few tobacco-chewing fellows have dribbled their spit into the bucket, the stuff is foul enough to choke a horse.

I'd like to move up to a better job, but Pa says I

need "seasoning," and that being a "bucket boy" is a good start.

August 25

Today is Sunday, the only day of the week we get to ourselves. Most of the men are worn out from last night's celebrating and are still in bed. Those who hitched a ride into Julesburg are in the worst shape. Bill Flanagan, for one, begged Pa to shoot him this morning. "Put me out of my misery, Paddy," he moaned, and as green as his face was, I think he was only half kidding.

Ben Wharton invited me to go fishing in Lodgepole Creek, a little stream that runs alongside the railroad grade. He's got a couple of willow sticks that he uses for poles, but they work just fine. Since the fish all congregate in the pools when the water's low, we had pretty good luck. Ben told me how he loved to fish back in the mountains where he came from. "The Greenbrier River was my favorite place," he said. "You just touch the tip of your worm to the water, and a speckled-sided brook trout—they's as pretty as a fresh-opened flower at dawn—will shoot out from under a rock or a cut bank."

Sitting beside that dusty little stream made me lonesome for home and for real water. Back in Chicago, me and my brother, John, could walk over to Lake Michigan and catch all the fish we wanted. My mother was always proud when we brought home a nice stringer of walleyes for supper. Even though we were little fellows and couldn't help dragging the fish in the dust, she never scolded us once, even when she was feeling poorly from her baby troubles, which came along pretty regular. The rivers were good fishing, too, especially in the spring. During spawning time, we could spear as many as we wanted right out of the Chicago River.

August 26

This afternoon, just when I'd brought the head spikers their water, there was a short stoppage in the tracklaying. The back iron men had accidentally dumped a pile of rails off their cart, and Pa was helping them load back up. While the spikers were waiting, I picked up a new maul that was lying beside the tracks. It had a smooth hickory handle and a shiny steel head.

One of the spikers, a gentle, red-haired fellow named Michael Kennedy, said, "Give it a swing if you like."

I must have looked hesitant, because he said, "Go ahead. There's nothing to it." He even walked over and started a spike for me with two quick taps.

When he handed me the maul, I got up on my toes and swung as hard as I could. The maul grazed the head of the spike, and it flew sideways down the tracks. What's worse, the handle of the maul smacked across the rail and broke clean off.

With my mouth hanging open, I stared at the shattered hickory in my hands. I expected Mac O'Grady to step forward and throttle me. Instead, the whole spiking crew burst out laughing. "And I thought it was the Injuns who was dangerous," said a man in a Union army cap who bent to pick up my spike, which had ricocheted off the toe of his boot. When he tossed it back toward me, they laughed even more. I'm glad Pa wasn't around.

Michael Kennedy was the only fellow who showed any kindness, and even he was grinning. Kennedy explained my mistake, saying, "You've got to keep your eye on the target and swing smooth. Otherwise you'll be sending a maul to the carpentry shop every time you miss."

The fellows were still chuckling as I picked up my buckets and headed back to the wagon.

August 27

Pa heard about me breaking the spike maul. Mac O'Grady teased him at breakfast about having a son "not worth his salt." But my pa spoke right up and told him to shut his mouth or he'd shut it for him.

As we were walking off to start our day's work, Pa

took me aside and said, "Never mind that O'Grady. He's Tipperary trash. You may not be strong enough to wield a spike maul yet, but be patient. I was a skinny pup, too, when I was your age."

I looked up at all six foot three inches of Pa. He was a square-shouldered giant of a man with a giant temper to match. It was impossible for me to imagine him being either patient or small, and he knew it. When he saw the doubt in my eyes, he smiled. "Well, maybe I wasn't quite as slim as you"—he clapped me on the back and gave my shoulder a quick squeeze—"but you'll come into your own sooner than you know."

After I took my seat beside Ben and we drove his wagon all the way to the water tank, I could still feel the spot that Pa had squeezed. Lord save the man who ever gets in the way of Patrick Sullivan's fist.

August 28

I had a strange experience this evening. Pa and I were walking to the dining car when we heard a buzzing sound. We stopped, and the buzzing got so loud, it almost hurt. The next thing I knew, the sky went black, and Pa whispered, "Locusts." We ducked back into the tent just in time.

I peeked through the flap as a big bunch of them

swooped down and started munching up the dry grass stalks. As sparse as the grass was, I could hear those hoppers chewing as they worked their way along. Fellows who'd been caught outside were slapping at their shirtsleeves and collars as they ran for cover.

I had seen big swarms of grasshoppers before—a neighbor once paid John and me a dime to clear out his corn patch—but I never would have believed there could be this many in one place. Even after the best part of them had moved on, they were still so thick on the rails that when an engineer tried to pull his locomotive forward, the wheels spun like they'd been greased.

I really wish John could have been here to see it, because telling it in a letter isn't going to be the same. I sure do miss him.

August 29
Antelope, Nebraska (mile 451)

Today we reached Kimball. I noticed that the assistant engineers and foremen talk a lot about the total miles of track the company has laid. I asked Pa why, and he says that depending on the difficulty of the terrain, the government pays the Union Pacific $16,000 to $48,000 for every mile of track they finish. With that much money at stake, I can see why there's so much excitement over the race between us and another railroad called the Central Pacific. They started laying track east from Sacramento, and they want to beat us to the Rockies in the worst way. So its the U.P. versus the C.P., and we're not only fighting for money in the bank but for pride. We aim to prove we're the best.

We are exactly 451 miles from Omaha. (They measure from Omaha because that's the place where the U.P. first started laying track two years ago.) According to Pa, we're not even halfway done, and he says the toughest and meanest country is yet to come.

Dead grasshoppers crunch under our boots wherever we go.

September 5

During some slack time this morning, Mr. Casement asked me and Ben to help clean out a passenger car that some visiting dignitaries had been using. They call it the "Lincoln car" because it belonged to the president before the Union Pacific bought it. I've never seen such a fancy interior. The upholstery was plush green, and the whole car was decorated with crystal chandeliers and gold-trimmed mirrors and velvet curtains. The ceiling and walls were a rich, dark-grained wood that was polished and carved like furniture.

As we cleaned up the cigar butts and the spilled whiskey, I told myself that if anyone ever invited me to stay in a fine place like this, I would be polite enough to pick up after myself.

I got a letter from John today. Pa says the mail is slow to arrive sometimes here at the end of the track. John did a lot of complaining, but it still felt good to hear from him.

> *Dear Sean,*
>
> *Thanks for your letter.*
>
> *You are lucky to be working on the railroad now that it's canning season back here. I've picked enough beans for Aunt Katie to put up ten thousand quarts. It'd be different if I liked beans, but I gag just looking at all those jars lined up in the cellar. I don't care whether beans are fresh or string dried or canned, they taste awful to me. As you know, I don't mind helping with the sweet pickles, but Aunt Katie prefers to put up mainly dills. Next we'll be making applesauce and pressing cider.*
>
> *Have you seen any Indians? Are there lots of buffalo out there? The boys at school say that the big bulls chase the trains, and whenever they get a chance they hook fellows with their*

horns and trample them into the ground.

By the way, school has started up again, and my teacher is a big crab.

Your bean-picking brother,
John

September 15

We've just had our first snowstorm. Growing up in Chicago, I thought I was used to cold, but the wind can really rip out here. A little skim of ice even formed on the pond beside the tracks. It looks like winter crowds right in on the tail end of summer on these plains.

I can tell by the way that Ben has been rubbing his bad arm lately that the cold really pains him, but he never complains.

One good thing about this weather—the fellows drink a lot less water.

September 18

I've been promoted. At least my pa calls it a promotion and tells me he's real proud. He says that the job of water carrier is reserved for the youngest and greenest boys on the railroad, and this is a step up. But I think my new job is lots worse. My official title is "dish swabber." As a water carrier, I got to go up and down the roadbed in Ben's wagon, but now, except when we haul lunch out to the men at noon, I am stuck in the kitchen and dining cars.

A dish swabber does exactly what you'd guess—he cleans the dishes. But it's not like a normal dishwashing job. The work train moves so often that the plates and cups would fall out of cupboards. To make things simple, they nailed the tin plates right down to the tables. Just one nail in the middle was all it took. It was our head cook's idea—his name is Jimmy Flynn—and he's proud of what he calls his "permanent set table."

So instead of bringing the plates to the dishwasher, I bring myself to the plates. They give me a bucket of water and a rag, and I have to hustle up and down the line, wiping off each one as quick as I can. I've got to work fast because our dining car seats two hundred fellows, and they eat in shifts. When a new group is ready to sit down, the fellows don't want to wait so much as a fraction of a second, or I hear about it.

September 19

I could barely open my eyes this morning. Though everyone else gets to sleep until the bell rings at half past five, the kitchen crew has to roll out of bed at four o'clock to get breakfast started. I can't get used to being up when it's still near pitch dark outside.

What makes it even worse is that everyone wakes up hungry and ready to growl if their food isn't waiting for them. The heavy sleepers are the orneriest, because the foremen have to kick them out of bed. The bosses aren't shy about using their boots to get the laggards moving, either. I've even seen them pitch rocks at fellows who are sleepin' in tents that are set up on the roofs of the cars.

First we put out big buckets of coffee — the men just serve themselves by dipping their tin cups in — and then we lay out platters piled up with bread and huge plates of meat. The fellows stick their forks into whatever happens to be close by, so I keep my hands clear. The amount of food that the men eat is enormous. It's like trying to feed a herd of cattle.

Since Mother and Aunt Katie both prided themselves in setting a neat table, it's hard for me to get used to such bad manners. When the men are done, they just clomp off without so much as a good morning or a thank you for the grub. Some of them even step right across the table on their way out the door. O'Grady left a dirty boot print right beside his plate today, and you can guess who had to clean it up.

September 20

General Casement has everything on the Union Pacific organized like an army. Pa says Mr. Casement treats the men on his work train like the soldiers he commanded during the war. Though it's hard to describe, there's something about Mr. Casement that makes men want to follow him. And it's more than just his bullwhip and six-shooter that gets people's attention.

His goal is two miles of track a day, and he pays us double every time we make it. Since the boys are already making more than a dollar a day, the promise of those bonuses keeps them flying. Pa is especially glad for the extra money because he is sending most of his pay home. They started me at $18 per month.

General Casement gets riled anytime the work slows down. This afternoon we were hauling the lunch out to the men when Ben Wharton's wagon, which was directly in front of us, got stuck in a deep rut. While Ben urged his team to pull, me and two other fellows pushed on the wagon, but it wouldn't budge.

Ben was going to get some wood to block up the wheel when Casement rode by. He swung down off his horse, saying, "Let's get on with it, lads." Then he bent down and put his shoulder to the back of the wagon. I was just thinking how's a little fellow like that gonna help when the wheel popped out of that hole so fast that the three of us fell face first into the dirt. Before we could even dust ourselves off, the general was back on his horse and gone.

Ben had a good laugh over that.

September 21

Tonight after supper, I asked Pa how a man as small as Casement could be so strong, and he said it was more a matter of mind than muscle. "When a thing needs to happen," Pa said, "he wills it to be."

"You mean like in Julesburg last summer?" Bill Flanagan interrupted.

Normally I hate when Bill butts in, but when Pa tried to hush him up, I got curious. It took a few questions on my part, but I finally pried out of him what had happened in Julesburg.

So many U.P. men were getting busted up in town—it was right near the end of the line back then—that Casement decided to clean out the ruffians. Julesburg had become a refuge for every wanted man in the territory, and the local law was afraid to do anything about it. So Casement armed a crew of men and took them into town. (Bill admitted that he went along, but my pa wouldn't say one way or the other.) When Casement asked the outlaws and gamblers to clear out of town, the surly rascals laughed right in his face. That was a mistake. There was a gun battle, and after the smoke cleared, General Casement had thirty men hung. Those who were still alive were begging for a chance to pack their bags and clear out of town.

September 22

I can't put that Julesburg story out of my mind. Thirty hangings in one afternoon? It's hard enough for me to think back on the dead man's face that I saw last month without gettin' the shakes, but I can't imagine thirty bodies swaying in the wind.

I sure hope Pa wasn't there.

September 24

The longer I work in the kitchen, the more amazed I am that somebody doesn't die of an awful disease. Nothing is clean. And that includes the plates I'm supposed to be swabbing. I do the best job I can, but by the time I get to the end of the table, I know I'm leaving chunks of food. Some of the guys wipe their plates off with their sleeves before they heap them full, but most of 'em dig right in.

I feel bad, but with two hundred hungry track men hollering at me, I can't clean any better. The sad thing is that the dirtiest spot on every plate is right smack in the middle, because my rag is always catching on those nails. With all the slimy stuff that oozes off my rag, who knows what could be growing under those nail heads?

September 26

I'm tired of getting up so early.

October 1

I never thought I'd consider butchering cleaner than cooking, but I do now. To get out of that filthy dish swabbing, I volunteered to help with the meat cutting. And I can honestly say that hacking up steers is a blamed sight more appealing to me than wiping crusty food off those plates.

October 4

I suspect that every job, no matter how good it might look to everyone else, has a bad side. Anyone could guess the bad side of butchering, but there is something worse than all the blood and guts. That something is named Jimmy Flynn.

October 6

It's Sunday, but I don't feel much like writing because my hands are cramped up pretty bad. Pulling the hides off those big beef cattle, even when you get 'em fresh, really wears you out.

Jimmy Flynn is not a clean person.

October 8

What I said the other day is too polite. Jimmy Flynn is a pig. And I mean pig in the worst pig-rooting-on-a-manure-pile sense. Though Jimmy has a beautiful mustache that he waxes up and twists into tiny curls at the ends, that's as far as his good looks go.

He wears a dirty apron that's stained black with blood and who knows what else, and he refuses to take it off. Today one of the other helpers whispered to me, only half joking, that he heard Jimmy slept in that apron.

The rest of Jimmy Flynn is just as ugly as his apron. His hair sticks straight out from under his flat-crowned hat, his shirttail is always flying out behind him, and his boots are always dragging through the slop on the floor of the car.

And you'd think a butcher would wash his hands, but I've never seen Jimmy go to the bucket and rinse himself off even once.

October 10

If some fellows have chips on their shoulders, Jimmy Flynn has a huge pile of bricks sitting on his. He's just a little guy, and I suspect he's always grumping and growling at the world because everyone is taller than he is.

Being that my pa is a big, broad-shouldered fellow and I lean toward the thin side, Jimmy ribs me a lot about being adopted. "You're as skinny as a twenty-pound rail," he says. We measure the size of the rails by pounds per yard, and a twenty-pound rail is real puny. "Patrick must've got you from the leprechauns."

Teasing is one thing, but I don't like him making leprechaun jokes. That reminds me too much of my mother. Because whenever my brother and me got to fighting and wouldn't quit, she'd say, "Stop now, you rascals. It's leprechauns that come to get bad little boys."

October 15

As ugly and mean as Jimmy Flynn is, I have to admit that he can wield a knife like no one else. He starts by taking a half-dozen quick passes across his butcher's steel, and then without breaking that rhythm, he goes right to work. His blade is a silver blur when he slabs out steaks or chops up stew meat. The amazing thing is that he gabs the whole time and never looks at his work. I keep expecting him to take off his hand, but he's never slipped once. A man can still hope, though.

October 21

Me and two other fellows were lifting a side of beef off a meat hook this morning when it slipped out of our hands. It knocked me right down, and Jimmy laughed his head off. "You gonna fetch that meat, boy? Or are you gonna dance with it?"

I wish someone would cut out that man's tongue.

Wyoming

October 26
Hillsdale, Wyoming (mile 496)

Though we are officially in the Dakota Territory now, most of the men call this place "Wyoming" because everyone expects it will be made into the Wyoming Territory real soon.

Pa and all of the fellows brag that we will have no trouble beating the Central Pacific because their workers are mainly Chinese. Pa says, "Those runty Celestials ain't got a chance of beating us County Cork boys." "Celestials" is a name they use for the Chinese because lots of the fellows call China the Celestial Empire.

I know my mother would've hated to hear him going on like that about the Chinese, but if you can believe it, Pa is polite compared to most of the guys. The other day, Bill Flanagan heard about a terrible accident that killed several Chinese C.P. workers. It sounded like they were hanging over a mountainside in a wicker basket to set a black powder charge when they were blown right off the face of the cliff. Bill just laughed and said, "That'll learn 'em. A little stiffer charge mighta blowed them heathens all the way back to China where they belong."

Talk about heathens — Bill's got a Bible above his bunk, but I've never seen him open it. I suspect that he can't even read, because whenever Pa is reading something out loud from the newspaper, Bill listens real careful. Then he spouts the stuff off to someone else like he read it himself, but he always gets everything all tangled up. I swear that man is dumber than a fence post.

October 28

A fight broke out between Bill Flanagan and another Irishman today. It happened during supper after a hard day. Tempers were short, and a man called Dailey swore across the table at Bill. The next thing I knew, Bill was on his feet, and Dailey took a swing at him — a big roundhouse it was, but he missed. Since Bill is always shooting off his mouth, I was hoping that Dailey would bust him in the chops. But before you could blink, Bill gave the fellow a head butt that knocked him out cold. Dailey swayed for an instant, then he fell face forward into his coffee, spilling food and dishes all over the place.

"That's a Cork man for you," the fellow beside Bill called out, patting him on the back to congratulate him.

All this County Cork and Tipperary hate talk confuses me. I always thought an Irishman was an Irishman. I knew Pa and Bill hated the Indians, but I can't believe they hate other Irish. Why should Pa, who was born on the Chicago waterfront, care what county in Ireland someone came from?

November 1

This afternoon, I met a famous buffalo hunter named William Cody. He's nicknamed "Buffalo Bill." Since Cody supplies meat for all the workers on the Kansas-Pacific Railroad, he was trying to convince Jimmy Flynn that the U.P. could save a lot of money if they switched to buffalo steaks. Jimmy just laughed and told him that his boys won't tolerate anything but beef. I know that's true because Jimmy has tried serving both mule deer and antelope, and the fellows threatened to skin his hide every time.

After he and Jimmy joked a bit, Cody put on a shooting demonstration for us. He tossed three bottles into the air, drew out his six-shooter, and broke every one before they hit the ground. Then for the grand finale, he flicked an ace of spades into the air and drilled it right through.

I had never seen such a display of shooting and was real impressed until I talked to Pa. He just laughed and said that all those trick-shot artists load their cartridges with BBs instead of bullets. No wonder Buffalo Bill could put on such a show. Even my aunt Katie can bust a bottle with bird shot.

★ ★ ★

November 9
Archer, Wyoming

I cut myself this afternoon. It was a stupid mistake. We were slicing up steaks for supper, and Jimmy Flynn told me to hurry. "Those boys will be in here chewing on you, sonny, if you don't get some steaks ready pronto." I hurried so fast that my knife slipped. At first I didn't think it was too bad. But when I wiped my hand off on my apron, I could see that my palm was opened up pretty good. Though I did my best to hide it, Jimmy noticed the blood dripping onto the floor and got Pa. The whole time I was waiting, I couldn't help but think I was being punished for wishing all that bad luck on Jimmy. I felt even worse because Jimmy was kind to me for a change and never made any jokes.

I told Pa we could just wrap it up tight, but after one look, he said no. Since our company doctor was out tending to a man on the grading crew, Pa took me by wagon to Cheyenne. When I complained that he shouldn't bother, his lips got tight and he said, "I don't want to lose you, son."

We stopped at the doctor's office — the sign said, J. ADAMS, PHYSICIAN — and knocked on the door. A lady in a white smock answered, and Pa said, "We'd like to see the doctor."

She said, "That's me."

Not expecting a woman doctor, Pa stood there, not knowing what to say.

She laughed and said, "If the lad wants that bleeding stanched, you'd better bring him inside. I don't tend my patients in the street." Then she took me by my good hand and, looking down at the bloody bandage, added, "So what's this? A bullet hole or a bear bite?"

Her joking relaxed me, and though it was different meeting a lady doctor, Mrs. J. Adams did a fine job of sewing me back together. Pa stood off to the side the whole time, watching to see that she did everything right, but she was a big improvement over Doc Barnes back in Chicago, who never smiles and always has whiskey on his breath.

When she was done, she gave me a hug and made me promise to be more careful with "nasty bladed things" as she called them.

That hug made me lonesome for my mother in the worst way. It's funny how a little thing like a hug, or the look of a woman's bonnet, or the laughter of a lady—even if it's coming from the doorway of a saloon—can remind me of my mother. It's like for an instant, I forget she is gone, but before the thought is even done, it vanishes. It's almost as if a person has to die over and over again. Memories do that.

November 10

Ben stopped by and checked on me this evening. He teased me about not being able to tell the difference between my hand and a hunk of beefsteak, and he said that if I wasn't careful, I'd end up workin' as a one-armed mule skinner like him.

It felt good to laugh. Pa has been looking at me like he expects me to drop over dead any minute.

November 18
Cheyenne, Wyoming (mile 516.4)

With all the territory these tracks have covered so far, I can't believe that the engineers can measure the distance down to a fraction of a mile. But they claim that we are exactly 516 and 4/10 miles from Omaha.

There was a big celebration when the U.P. rolled into town. The local citizens had set up a speaker's stand with a big banner that read, THE MAGIC CITY GREETS THE TRANSCONTINENTAL RAILROAD. Eddy Street was lit with torches and kerosene lamps, and men with suits and stovepipe hats took turns making some long-winded speeches about "progress" and "the promise of the future."

Pa says that the population of Cheyenne is close to four thousand, though it was a just an empty bend on the Crow River a month ago. And he claims that every gambler and strumpet that got run out of Julesburg last summer has set up shop here.

I can't believe the crowds. Besides the brand-new depot, city hall, and two-story hotel, there are one hundred saloons all doing a booming business. Town officials have plans to build a church and a school, but by then the U.P. road builders will be long gone.

November 15

Real estate speculation in town is going wild. Lots that sold for $150 two months ago are bringing $1,000 and up.

November 17

Pa went into Cheyenne with Bill Flanagan last night and he never came back. He said that he needed to buy a bottle of liniment and wouldn't be long, but I waited and waited, and he never showed up.

I shuffled the cards a few times and tried playing a little solitaire. Then I went outside and paced up and down the tracks, wondering what I should do. Midnight came. The men started trickling back to the work train, but no one had any news of Pa.

I finally lay down on my bunk and dozed off, worried

that he'd been hurt or killed. A long while later, I woke to the sound of singing. I looked outside the tent, and there were Bill and Pa stumbling along arm in arm and soused to the gills.

I'd been proud of Pa for not drinking and gambling like the rest of the fellows, and I couldn't figure out why he'd gone and done it. But as he lifted the tent flap and looked me in the eye, he whispered, "I'm sorry, Sean, but it was me and Maggie's day, you know."

Then I remembered. November 17 was his anniversary. Next thing I knew, he was crying—not the usual kind of weeping of a drunk—just huge tears running down his cheeks and splashing onto his boots.

As Bill and I helped him into bed, he kept mumbling, "Me and Maggie's day . . . me and Maggie Montgomery Sullivan . . ."

This morning, Pa got up at his regular time, and to my surprise he showed no signs of last night's escapade. He simply patted me on the shoulder and said, "Sorry I kept you waiting last night, Sean. It won't happen again."

Then we went off to the dining car, and Pa downed his usual enormous breakfast.

★ ★ ★

November 20

We are stuck here in Cheyenne, waiting for supplies. My hand is stiff and sore, but the worst thing is the teasing. Jimmy Flynn is making up for being nice to me on the day I cut my hand. He never lets up, and I'm getting tired of jokes about boys who can't tell the difference between their hand and a side of beef.

General Casement is pacing a lot lately. Loads of fresh Irish workers are arriving daily—many straight from the old country—and there's nothing for them to do but drink Red Dog whiskey at a dollar a bottle and fight. There is so much violence in town that a local paper has started a column called "Last Night's Shootings." Half our work crews will be dead if the next shipment of rails isn't delivered soon.

Casement wants to lay the thirty-two-mile stretch to Sherman Summit before we quit for the winter. But that two-thousand-foot rise between here and the summit is bound to be tough going. Everyone is wondering how long the weather will hold.

November 22

It's gotten so cold that Pa and Bill and I have moved into the bunk car. Some of the fellows snore loud enough to rattle the roof boards. And all of them stink. Pa and

I still visit the bathhouse on Saturday to wash up, but most of the fellows are in too much of a hurry to run off to town to get drunk.

November 28

We celebrated Thanksgiving today with a fancier than usual meal. Along with our meat and potatoes, we had squash pie. I only got a little smidgen, but it was fine. I asked Pa why people are fussing over Thanksgiving lately, and he said that it was President Lincoln's doing. Though George Washington made Thanksgiving an official holiday, people had forgotten about it over the years. But once the Civil War ended, Lincoln decided that we'd better get busy again and show that we were thankful.

November 29

We finally started laying track toward the summit. I say "we" because I just got promoted to the grading crew. We work out ahead of the track men. The minute Mr. Casement asked for extra help, I jumped up quick as a whistle. And you can bet I didn't waste a lot of time saying good-bye to Jimmy Flynn.

When I told Pa about my new job, he was proud. "Pretty soon you'll be the chief engineer," he joked, "and bossing me around."

We are fast approaching eight thousand feet, and the higher we go, the colder it gets. My cut hand aches some, but it's knitted back together clean. Whenever I'm tempted to complain, I just remember what it was like being cooped up in the butcher car with ugly old Jimmy Flynn. I like working outside in the open air, even if it gets so cold that I lose all the feeling in my face.

Bleak gray clouds fill the passes, and the mountains are coated with frost plumes. The rails are so slick that the brakes on the trains barely hold. Our engineers just creep along, spreading sand on the rails with their sand pipes and hoping for the best. The fellows I feel most sorry for are the brakemen. They have to ride out in the open on top of the cars and crank down the big wheels that slow the trains. When they jump from car to car, it's easy for them to slip. I know of two men who fell between the cars this month alone.

It's easy for us graders to lose our footing, too. It was sleeting yesterday, and when I stepped on an icy rock without thinking, my feet flipped right out from under me. It was pure luck that I caught myself before I kissed the dirt, and the fellows had a good laugh. I was grateful that I didn't split my head open or skid off the side of the mountain like Seamus McGlynn did on Tuesday. He broke one arm and busted up his kneecap real bad.

December 1

General Casement has taken to wearing a tall fur cap. He looks just like a picture of a Russian Cossack that I saw in a magazine one time.

December 5

Pa is shaking his head a lot lately. In a rush to get as much track laid as he can, Mr. Casement is having the men set ties right on top of the frozen snow. (Pa says he's following the orders of the U.P. vice president Durant, who is a real pushy fellow.) Though the rails are going down fast, Pa says the whole job will have to be redone. He's worried that a train is going to slide off the mountain when the weather breaks next spring.

My hands have never been this cold. I am picking and shoveling as best I can, but it's tough to keep ahead of the track men. The dirt and rocks are frozen into such hard clumps that sparks fly off the tip of my pick.

December 25

For Christmas, Pa gave me a pair of wool socks and a heavy cap. He also gave me a new journal so I can start 1868 off fresh, and a copy of a new book called *Journey to the Center of the Earth*, by Jules Verne. It must have been a trick for him to get those books sent way out here. It will be a long while before book and stationery stores try to compete with these saloons. The clothes and book are nice, but the journal is special because it's not the sort of thing he would normally think to buy. I borrowed some thread from Bill and sewed it right into my old journal.

I bought Pa and John and Uncle Willy winter jackets, and I sent Aunt Katie a pretty scarf. I hope I got John a big enough size, because in his last letter he told me that Aunt Katie says he's "growing like a weed." Pa said I spent way too much, but I'm on full wages now—$35 per month—and since I'm not wasting my money on Red Dog whiskey like the rest of the fellows, I've got lots of spare cash.

December 31

The tracklaying is done for the year. We never made it to the summit, but we're within hollering distance. Pa says Mr. Casement plans on stocking up on rails and other materials through the winter and hitting the work hard come spring. He plans on hiring hundreds of more guys, too. I wonder how many miles a day he's going to expect out of us next year?

January 10, 1868

I've already read through my Jules Verne book twice. Though Bill Flanagan cusses me out for staying up late and wasting lamp oil, Pa tells him to leave me be. That book has got me dreaming about creatures living underneath the ground.

To pass the time, Bill and Pa have been telling war stories lately. Back in Chicago, Pa would just shake his head when John and I asked questions about the war. He wouldn't even say what battles he'd fought in. But I think it's good for him to talk it out. So he doesn't feel uncomfortable, I try to pretend I'm not listening.

Pa talked about the day "Old Tecumseh"—that was a nickname he used for his commander, General Sherman—ordered them to set fire to the city of Atlanta. "Fighting battles is one thing," Pa said, "but burning down all those people's homes took her a notch too far for me."

When Bill reminded Pa of Sherman's famous statement that "war is hell," Pa asked, "But why did he have to spend his whole life proving it was true?"

January 14

A big blizzard hit yesterday. All the trains have stopped because of the drifts. I feel like I have shoveled off five miles of track in the last two days.

The temperature is thirty below zero. I helped Ben feed and water his mules tonight because I know this weather is hard on both him and his animals.

January 17

I got letters from John and Aunt Katie thanking me for their Christmas presents. Aunt Katie warned me like she always does about staying away from the saloons—I suspect the people back in Chicago have heard about our wild, hell-on-wheels railroad towns. Even Uncle Willy surprised me by adding a little note to Katie's letter, telling me to be careful. As usual, John's letter was the most interesting.

Dear Sean,
  Christmas was fun back here in Chicago.
Your present was the best!
  Just before vacation, my class went on a
hayride. Bart Jenkins pushed Susie McDougall
off the wagon, and she broke her arm. Susie
fainted from the pain, and my teacher, Miss

Collins, got so upset that she fainted, too.
The driver had to lift them both up on the
wagon—we boys had to help with Miss Collins
as she is rather large—and drive us right back
to town. We were mad at Bart 'cause as soon
as Miss Collins woke up, we had to go back to
school and do our spelling. He spoiled our whole
day. Bart's dad tanned his hide good, and I
can't say that I blame him.

Wish you could be here 'cause Uncle Willy is
taking me ice fishing tomorrow. I'll try to hook
a big one for you.

Is it still snowing a lot out there?

Your brother,
John

January 20

I haven't cared to write lately because all I can think
about is the snow and the cold. When I am not shoveling
snow, I am piling up the materials that are arriving daily. It's boring to unload carloads of bolts and
switch plates and ties and rails, and it's dangerous,
too, because you can get your toes or fingers pinched
by the heavy iron.

Last night, Pa and Bill talked about the final months

of the Civil War and how General Sherman got meaner and meaner as the war dragged on. He cut what Pa called a "bloody path" all the way from Atlanta, Georgia, to the sea. When Bill said that Sherman's idea of war was to burn down every house and rip up every rail and kill every living creature in his path, all Pa could do was nod. "About the only thing I ever saw him spare was a hound dog," Pa said, his eyes misting over at the thought.

I'm glad that I've finally been able to hear about what Pa lived through. It helps me understand the blank stares he used to give us when he first got back from the war.

February 10

I know what it is to be mudsiller now. Actually, I know what it's like to be worse than a mudsiller—a no siller. I'm living in a sod hut at a place called Dale Creek. Since the tracklaying is on hold, they've sent Pa and me and two dozen other fellows ahead to a place called Dale Creek, where the U.P. needs to build a bridge fast. They say the Central Pacific is going great guns, and if we want to keep up, we've got to finish our tunnels and bridges on time. Otherwise our tracklayers will get held up.

The main timbers have been shipped in from Michigan, and there's already forty or fifty men here who've set up a portable sawmill to cut additional supports.

Everyone is living in mud-chinked log huts on the site. The walls look like normal log cabins with untrimmed ends. But the big problem is the flat sod roofs. They stop water about as good as a dish-swabbing rag.

February 12

We are sawing logs and bolting timbers together from dawn to dark. When I look at the span of Dale Creek Gorge—Pa says it's at least 600 feet long and 120 feet high—I can't imagine we'll ever finish this bridge on time.

My pants are so sticky with pine pitch that they could stand up by themselves.

Pa and I are both getting real lonesome for home. Last night, he promised me that we could invite John out to visit next summer. I'm writing him a letter this evening to tell him the good news.

February 18

I woke up this morning with a worm crawling across my upper lip. It startled me so bad that it took every ounce of my strength to keep from screaming. I'm not afraid of worms, mind you. Back home, John and I use 'em for fishing all the time. One summer, we even raised some big fat ones in a wooden box filled with coffee grounds and vegetable peelings. But waking up like that really spooked me.

When the fellows fire up the stove, stuff is always dripping down through the sod. A fat little slug fell in Pa's coffee yesterday, and as strong stomached as he is, he dumped that cup outside and didn't drink no more.

February 17

My journal has two big water spots on the cover. I always feel damp and dirty in this place. Pa says we'll be going back to the work train by the first week in March, and I can't wait.

March 10

I'm on the grading crew again. Pa teased me when we first got back from Dale Creek. "I heard Jimmy Flynn was looking for another helper," he said. I just about dropped in my tracks until I saw him grinning. The longer we are out here, the more relaxed Pa gets. It's hard for me to remember all the way back to before the war, but I'd have to say he's close to his old self. Aunt Katie sure knew best when she told Pa to come out here. And I sure am glad I got to come with him.

Enough snow has finally melted for us to start preparing the roadbed.

March 12

My grading crew boss is a silent fellow named Larry Coughlin. He is the perfect opposite of Jimmy Flynn. While Jimmy is always shooting off his mouth, Mr. Coughlin rarely speaks. He is all business and, unlike most of the men, his clothes are neat and he shaves every day. Coughlin wears a Union army cap pulled down low to shade his eyes, which are a steely blue.

Coughlin's main job is supervising the teamsters and, like Ben Wharton, he really knows how to handle the draft animals. Even the most stubborn mule—one of the fellows named her Sue, after his wife who ran off with a riverboat gambler—will turn and look right at him whenever he whistles. The problem with Coughlin is that he shows a lot more concern for the mules and horses than the men. I've seen him spend ten minutes soothing a spooked horse, and then send off a fellow who took a rock chip in the eye and was bleeding real bad with a wave of his hand and a "Go see the doc."

The first day I was assigned to Coughlin's crew, I told him my name was Sullivan. All he said was, "Irish, eh?" and handed me a shovel. He never told me where to go or what to do with it. Of course, it didn't take a genius to figure out what came next.

Our job is to cut away the high spots, shovel the fill into wagons, and dump it in the low places. Teams pull scraper blades behind us for the final leveling of the grade.

When the digging is rough, we have to use our picks. If that doesn't work, we blast. It's actually fun watching a charge go off. Not only do we get a little break from our work, but we get to watch some fine fireworks.

Pa swings by once in a while and tries to pretend that he isn't checkin' up on me. But I know better. He preached at me for two nights about how to protect myself during a blast. The trick is to fight the urge to duck your head at the powder flash. You've got to look straight up to dodge the material that's raining down. I'm glad Pa coached me, 'cause once a rock gets airborne, it's anybody's guess where it's going to land.

March 28

It feels great to have the sun back. I thought winter was never going to end, but a sudden warm spell has opened up the mountains. The south slopes are bare, and shoots of green grass and tiny wildflowers are popping up all over. I'm so happy to see everything coming back to life that I don't even mind the flies.

Pa and Bill and I are back in our tent.

March 25

The storm of all storms hit yesterday. It was scary how quiet it started. There was a soft breeze blowing out of the south, like it had all week. Summer looked to be so close that I was even thinking about trying a swim in the river.

Then, late in the afternoon, the breeze shifted over to the north. I didn't think anything of it until I heard the pitch of the wind change all of a sudden. We all leaned on our shovels and listened to the sound hit a high, whining note. A few minutes later the air turned icy cold, and there was a soft hiss of snow blowing down the mountain and across my boot tops.

By noon today, everything had stopped dead. Snow has drifted as deep as the telegraph poles, stalling the trains and completely burying the wagons. Ben told me that lots of livestock are missing.

April 1

It took us a week to shovel out from the blizzard. A stage was stranded for six days in the Cheyenne Pass, and the driver got frostbit so bad that the doc had to saw one of his legs off.

Tracklaying operations are going full tilt now.

Word is that Indian troubles have started up again back on the plains. Pa says he can't risk letting John visit us like we'd planned. I hate to write and tell him, but I have to.

April 5
Sherman Summit, Wyoming

We've reached the summit. Though it's plenty cold working on the grading crew, it's a big improvement over sod hut living.

Mr. Casement is pushing us already. No matter that the ground is still too frozen for picks. No matter that the air is so thin that we get nosebleeds, Casement's railroad will be built.

Pa is shaking his head at the shoddy tracklaying. All we did to prepare the grade was scrape away a little snow and blast a chunk of frozen rock here and there. Sometimes it felt like the tie setters were chasing us right up the mountain. Pa says that all this track will have to be repaired before the first train can make it through to San Francisco.

Counting the new men who were recruited over the winter, there's now over five thousand track men and graders working for the U.P. Ben Wharton says it takes one thousand mule-and-horse teams hauling full time to keep everyone busy.

April 11

The Dale Creek Bridge almost blew down in a storm the other day. Pa talked to an engineer named Hezekiah Bissell, who said that a big wind came up, and the whole bridge started swaying from side to side. His crew just stared as it rocked back and forth.

With some fast talking, Bissell finally convinced a few fellows to crawl out onto the bridge and attach some ropes. They had to stake a half-dozen lines before the bridge finally stopped swaying.

It gives me the chills to know that we are going to drive our work train over that trestle any day now.

April 12

Since Pa was feeling bad today—it would have been my mother's thirty-fourth birthday—I asked him if he wanted to go fishing. We borrowed Ben's poles and hiked up a fork of Dale Creek until we found a little pool. Pa never said anything about what day it was. He mainly talked about a stubborn fellow he had on his crew. Then, just before dark, he caught a nice trout using a cricket for bait. Instead of keeping it like I thought he would, he set the fish back in the shallows.

As it flicked away with a splash of its tail, Pa smiled and rinsed his hands off in the clear water. He looked at the purple mountains to the north and wrapped up his line. He reached out and put his arm around my shoulders. "This was a fine idea, son," he said. "There's nothing better than wild country to clear a man's mind." Then, as we turned back down the trail, he added, "I know your mother would have loved the look of these hills."

April 14

Today was the third anniversary of President Lincoln's assassination. The men who served in the Union army were more quiet than usual.

April 22

The Dale Creek Bridge is ready for a test run tomorrow. To me, it looks like a six-hundred-foot-long crisscross of toothpicks. Pa says they aren't going to let a train go any faster than four miles per hour, but if I had the choice, I'd rather climb down our side of the gorge and hike back up the other hill than ride over that flimsy trestle.

April 23

I never thought we'd make it, but the work train inched across the Dale Creek Bridge today. Bissell's men had left their guy ropes in place, and they pulled as tight as a set of banjo strings as the steel wheels of our flatcar creaked out onto the trestle. I felt the bridge timbers flex under the load and I waited for the ropes to pop. Would it be better to jump or just close my eyes and hang on tight?

After we made it to the other side, I thought about what the U.P. would have done if that feeble excuse for a trestle had given out. I bet they would have used us all for fill and carted in some extra dirt to level things off.

April 24

Indians raided a camp near Dale Creek. They killed two men, wounded four, and drove off a dozen head of stock. Back on Lodgepole Creek, two off-duty U.P.

men were attacked. One, named Bill Edmundson, ran a mile back to the station with four arrows sticking out of him. His buddy, Torn Cahoon, was scalped but, like Bill Thompson, he survived.

The U.P. has filled the space in the walls of their coaches and cabooses with sand to protect them from rifle fire. These days, Pa is sleeping with his loaded Colt right beside him. I suspect he's more concerned about protecting me than himself.

May 3

They are still trying to shore up the Dale Creek Bridge. Two carpenters fell to their deaths yesterday.

May 16

We just heard that the impeachment of President Andrew Johnson failed by a single vote. For the last week the telegraph wires have been humming with news of Johnson's trial. Though nobody out here seems to think a whole lot of Johnson, they agree with Bill Flanagan's opinion: "He ain't no Lincoln, but he deserves better than what those scalawags in Congress wanted to give him." Sometimes even Bill gets lucky and makes sense.

May 30

Congress has just declared a new holiday called Decoration Day to honor the soldiers who were killed in the war. It's just like those politicians to be trumping up the charges on President Johnson one day, and then declaring a national celebration the next.

June 8
Laramie, Wyoming (mile 573)

The days are getting warmer all the time. We've just hit a pretty stretch of the Laramie River that runs along the western edge of the Black Hills. A big flat plain lies ahead. The grading has been a picnic here compared to what we had back at Sherman Summit. Things are going so smooth that even Coughlin pushes back his army cap and admires the scenery once in a while.

I know I shouldn't complain after that long, ugly winter, but the sun sure gets hot on these western slopes. Lots of fellows have taken to wearing Mexican sombreros. My favorite part of the whole day is the few minutes I get after supper to take a swim. On the hottest days even Pa takes a dip. The fellows all have a good laugh when Pa takes a running start and leaps out into the river. Two hundred and twenty pounds of track boss can sure kick up a splash!

June 12

I got a letter from John today.

> Dear Sean,
>   How's life in the West? I am excited that
> school will finally be out next week. Bobby
> Williams and his pa and Uncle Willy and I are
> going camping on the Rock River. Billy's been
> there twice before and he says that though it
> is a long wagon ride, it is worth it because the
> fishing is so good. Being that hardly anyone goes
> up there, we should have the place to ourselves.
>   It is too bad that I won't be able to visit you
> this summer, but I wouldn't want to get killed
> by the Indians. According to the papers, the
> bullets are flying out there. How many times
> have you been shot at?
> Your fishing champion brother,
> John

Boy, would a summer vacation feel good about now.

June 14

It's Sunday. Pa and Ben Wharton and I went fishing this
afternoon. We didn't have any luck, but it was good to

see Pa relax. Ben started reminiscing about the war, telling about the day when he'd suddenly been moved to the front lines. When Ben mentioned a battle near Chattanooga, Tennessee, Pa joined right in without tensing up like he usually does. They were surprised to discover that they'd been on opposite sides in the very same battle.

As they discussed the layout of the field and where they'd been standing, they realized they'd probably been shooting at each other. "Lordy, Sean"—Ben turned to me—"if I'd a had two good arms, I mighta shot your papa dead."

He and Pa had a good laugh over that, but I really couldn't see the humor.

I always figured that Ben went home on leave after his arm was shot off. The Union army is lucky that the Confederates didn't have more soldiers like Ben on their side.

June 20

For the past week we've been on an easy stretch of grading. General Casement is pleased that the track is going down so fast. I can tell because though he has the same gruff face as always, I heard him whistling as he rode by our crew yesterday.

The boys were sitting around a campfire this afternoon, singing and clog dancing and sipping whiskey like they sometimes do on a Sunday, when a couple of trappers stopped by on their way to Medicine Bow. They warmed their coffee on our fire and ended up spending the night. They told us tales about faraway places like Bozeman and Missoula. One of those fellows was carrying a Hawken rifle that looked ten feet long. He claimed he could "shoot the eyelash off a mosquito at a hundred yards." Those fellows slept right out in the open and, by the time I got up for breakfast, they had saddled their horses and were gone.

July 1
Carbon, Wyoming (mile 656)

They call this place "Carbon" because there's a big coal deposit near here. Since the price of wood is up to $100 a cord on the plains, the coal will really help the U.P. save money. They are already busy converting the locomotives.

July 11

Since the grading was getting boring, I volunteered for what Coughlin called a new "detail" this morning. I figured that any job would be a welcome change of pace from dirt work.

Boy, was I mistaken. When I stepped forward, Coughlin pulled out a rusty old navy six-shooter and a box of cartridges from his haversack. "Go hunt down some snakes," he said.

When I just stood there, he looked irritated and said, "Get on, now."

After he walked off, I asked one of the other fellows what Coughlin meant. With a grin he explained that so many rattlesnakes were spooking the animals that the boss wanted someone to walk out ahead of the crew and clear out the snakes.

My first thought was, that'll teach me to not volunteer without knowing what I'm in for. But when I remembered that I could still be working for Jimmy Flynn, I decided I was one for two in the volunteering department.

July 13

I'm a lousy shot with that navy six. Though I can knock a can off a fence post at fifty yards with a rifle, I've never been able to hit a blessed thing with a six-shooter. That's not so bad when you're target shooting, but snakes are a bit trickier—they bite back.

Pa thinks Coughlin should shoot his own snakes, but I told him that it's my fault for volunteering.

July 14

At least my daily snake-hunting duties are short. My job is to check the grade each morning. Most of the time there's only a little rattler or two, and they slink off before I can even lift my gun. When I do run into a big one, I've learned to creep real close before I fire. But I can guarantee you that I'm aiming the whole time I walk forward, and I squeeze that trigger as soon as I hear the first rattle.

I actually feel a little sorry for the snakes. Like the buffalo, they've had this country to themselves for longer than any of us know. Now just because we've decided to build a railroad, we expect them to clear out of our way.

The one good thing about my hunts is that they've helped me appreciate my pick-and-shovel work. Though it might be hot and dirty filling the wagons, it's relaxing compared to snake patrol.

July 19
St. Mary's, Wyoming (mile 679)

We just got to a big tunnel. It's a two-hundred-foot-long sandstone cut that a crew of Mormons has been drilling and blasting for several months. The U.P. contracted with the head of the Mormon Church—his name is Brigham Young—to supply ties and timbers and do 120 miles of grading around Ogden, Utah. For now, we have to build our tracks around the tunnel because the rock is so crumbly that they have to timber the whole thing.

Pa and I peeked inside, and you couldn't pay me enough money to slave away like those tunnel rats do. It's hard to breathe in all the dust, and as soon as you step away from the yellow light of the kerosene lamps, you might as well be inside a coffin.

I haven't talked to any of the Mormons yet, but the fellows say that some of them have a dozen wives. I can't see how one man could keep track of that many ladies, much less keep them all happy. My uncle Willy back in Chicago has his hands full with only one woman, and I know that Pa still considers himself married to his Maggie.

July 21
Benton, Wyoming (mile 696)

This is the driest and dustiest place I've ever seen. When I toss a shovelful of dirt into the air, I end up eating half of it. I get so lonesome for the rivers and lakes back home, I'd give anything for a cool Lake Michigan breeze. I was hoping we'd find greener country soon, but General Casement has scouted seventy miles ahead, and he told Pa that it gets even worse. "It's the meanest place I've ever seen," he said. Considering how tough Casement is, that makes me plenty uneasy.

It's amazing how fast Benton, the latest hell-on-wheels town, is going up. The fellows have the building down pat. There's already twenty saloons and five dance halls. Some are ragged tents like we're used to seeing, but lots of the storefronts are being delivered straight from Chicago. They build them back East and ship them out here on flatcars. A few of the buildings are even painted with brick patterns that look almost like the real thing. They say a half-dozen men with hammers and screwdrivers can put up a city block in a single day.

Bill Flanagan says that one frame tent is a hundred feet long and has a mirror-backed bar, cut-glass goblets, gilt-framed pictures, and a band playing day and night. He joked that the paint hadn't even dried on the joint before they were serving up their "road poison." That's Bill's name for the cheap whiskey that they pass off on the U.P. workers. I thought that was pretty funny.

July 22

There's a whole bunch of newspapermen hanging around camp tonight. Pa said they never left him alone one minute all day because they are studying "tracklaying science." Though they like to refer to themselves as "editorial gentlemen," Pa calls them "nosy print hacks." He told one fellow off after supper when he wouldn't stop questioning him. "Can't you let a man rest?" he said. "The only science to this job is hard work and sweat."

Pa says that the U.P.'s advertising agency brings the reporters out here in plush railcars and pays all their expenses and gives them fancy meals just so they'll say nice stuff about the railroad. If that's true, I wonder if I can believe anything I read in the papers.

The price of water in Benton is up to ten cents a bucket. The people have to haul it all the way from the North Platte River, and that's five long, dusty miles away. Every well they've dug has come up dry so far. If they don't find water soon, this town may not last long.

July 24
Rawlins, Wyoming

There's a pretty little spring here that gushes right out of bare rock. Pa said that General Dodge discovered it on his first survey trip. It is a marvel to look at a flowing pool of water in this dry country.

To the west, the land is totally flat. There isn't a hint of a hill or a hummock as far as I can see. It's like God took a giant rolling pin to this landscape. I never thought I could miss trees so much.

July 25

I found out another reason why we've had so many newspapermen around lately. Pa took me into Benton for supper tonight, and we saw a crowd of men in army uniforms and fancy suits in front of the hotel. One fellow was even wearing a stovepipe hat and a cape. As we passed by, Pa tipped his cap, and said, "Evening, General."

When the men began climbing into a stagecoach, Pa pointed out a short man in a white hat with a dark beard and close-set eyes. "That's Ulysses S. Grant," he whispered. Then he explained that the fellow he'd spoken to was none other than General William Tecumseh Sherman, the man he'd served under during the war. Though Sherman was tall, he had a thin nose and the pale, tired face of an undertaker.

After they rode off, I asked Pa how a plain-looking fellow like Sherman could lead thousands of soldiers into battle. "Did you get a good look at his eyes?" he asked, and when I shook my head, all he said was, "If you ever look him straight in the eye, you'll know."

July 27

Mr. Casement told Pa that Grant and Sherman were passing through Benton the other night on their way to a big meeting at Fort Sanders. They hope to straighten out the financial mess that Durant has got the U.P. into and work out a peace treaty with Red Cloud at the same time. I wish them luck.

According to the papers, Congress just created the Wyoming Territory. Names are funny things. People have been calling this country "Wyoming" for years and years, yet it took Congress this long to finally catch up and make it official.

July 28
The Red Desert, Wyoming

It feels like we've reached the end of the earth. I can't believe the dust. Every night when I go to bed, I tell myself that this bleakness can't go on — that I'll wake up to find a pretty green valley over the next hill — but each morning the same dead land stretches on. Empty white sky. A bleak gray horizon. Ankle-deep alkali everywhere.

The dust is as fine as flour, and it gets between your teeth and up your nose and in your ears. You can't spit or swallow without tasting the bitterness.

The only half-pretty thing are the buttes. Tall, striped spires of red sandstone, they look like the Lord just plunked them down without any plan. At least they save a fellow from going crazy from the sameness.

I talked with Ben Wharton today, and he says that ten thousand draft animals and ten thousand workmen are now strung out along the U.P. roadbed. A constant cloud of dust hangs over us.

It hurts Ben to see the animals suffer in the heat. Six mules died one day last week. When they drop in their tracks, the mule skinners just untangle the lines and roll the bodies off to the side for buzzard bait.

Quite a few men have died from heatstroke, too. The only difference between the way the U.P. treats them and the mules is that the men get shallow graves. The chaplain says a little service, and the burying is done so quick that you've barely got time to get your hat back on before the grave is being mounded up. Sometimes they stick a board in the ground for a marker, but I don't think most of the fellows care one way or the other. A lot of them have been wandering since the war ended and don't have any relations left. A fellow named Donnelly, who died yesterday, asked to have the handle of a spike maul driven into the ground at his head. I heard O'Grady say that it was a waste of good hickory, but the other boys told him to shut his yap.

Though I can't understand why, a few fellows ask to be laid out right under the roadbed. A buddy of Ben's named Louis, whose chest was crushed by a wagon wheel and died real slow, said he wanted to be buried "right beneath those sleepers." "Sleepers" is another name we give to the ties.

Life is cheap out here in the desert. Your luck can run out at any minute. Even Pa is complaining about the heat.

I haven't seen a tree or a shrub or a blade of grass for two weeks.

August 1

My hands are getting so rough and calloused from all the picking and shoveling that they feel like sandpaper. When I itched a fly bite on my chin this afternoon, I felt some beard stubble. Pa says it won't be long before I'm shaving.

Today we passed a broken-up wagon box, and a pile of oxen bones that were picked clean of every bit of hide and hair.

★ ★ ★

August 10

We now have to haul our water fifty miles. It takes a full time crew to keep the big tanks on the flatcars filled.

The only good thing about this place is that it's too hot and dry for rattlesnakes, so Coughlin has canceled my morning scouting.

August 11

A fight broke out between the graders and the track-layers today. The track men have been pushing the grading crew lately, and bad feelings have been building. It's so easy for them to lay their rails on these flats that we can't stay ahead of them.

It started after lunch. The chuck wagon had just left, and the graders were busy moving their equipment. When one of our mule skinners didn't pull his scraper ahead fast enough to suit Mac O'Grady, he shouted, "Clear those nags out of the way so we men can get to work."

That really set the graders off. Their heads all wheeled, and a tough fellow called Frank Stranahan spit in the dirt and cursed O'Grady.

Next thing I knew, both groups were charging each other with their fists cocked. Hats were flying, and mules were jerking white-eyed at their bits. No one even noticed when an unbraked wagon rattled off on its own.

I was so stunned by the sound of a fist cracking into the jaw of a man next to me that I barely had time to duck a punch thrown at my head.

Casement cracked his bullwhip over the heads of the men, but they wouldn't back off until he finally emptied his six-shooter into the air. Though they grumbled at one another for the rest of the day, there were no more fisticuffs.

After dinner those same men were sharing a drink of whiskey and chuckling over their blackened eyes. As they laughed at their own foolishness, I couldn't help but think back to how bull-raging mad they were. If they hadn't thrown down their spike mauls and shovels before they went at it, I know there would've been someone dead on the tracks.

August 15

Mr. Casement is getting fed up with the excursionists. I think he hates them even more than Pa, and that's saying a heap. You'd think they'd leave us alone way out here, but just when we think we've seen the last of them, a new lot shows up at the end of the track. It's always the same sort, too—professors and fancy ladies and reporters and company officials all dressed up and itching to see the tracklayers at work so they can go back East and brag to everyone that they got a firsthand view of the modern wonder of the world—the Transcontinental Railroad.

"Useless gawkers," I heard Casement call them today.

August 20
Creston, Wyoming (mile 737)

According to the engineers, we've just laid our tracks across the Continental Divide. But it is still so flat that if the surveyors hadn't told us that we'd reached the place where two watersheds meet, I never would have guessed.

Casement is getting his two miles a day and then some. I got a letter from John last week, but things have been moving so fast around here that it took me until tonight to write back.

September 1

We laid sixty-five miles of track last month, but Pa says Durant is pushing for more. Rumors are that the C.P. is going even faster than we are. Though the mountains held the C.P. back a long time, the fellows say that they've reached a flat desert in Nevada and are going great guns.

The men are quick to shoot their mouths off. Tonight at supper, Bill Flanagan said, "No bunch of Chinamen is going to show us up," and everyone nodded their head.

September 6

Sunday. The days are getting shorter, but Casement isn't letting a little thing like darkness slow us down. We are working by moonlight, and when the moon isn't out, we string lamps along the grade. Sometimes we light piles of sagebrush to help see our way. The smoke bums my eyes, and it's hard to breathe when the wind is wrong.

One day last week, our crews worked from dawn to dusk and put down six miles of track.

"That'll show 'em," everyone said, but a few days later we heard that the C.P. had laid seven miles in only fourteen hours.

September 18

I got a letter from John today. He took a whole page to describe his geography teacher and, as usual, he cheered me up.

> *Dear Sean,*
>
> *School has started up again, and you are sure lucky that you are working on the rail-road instead of doing these dumb lessons. We've got a new geography teacher named Mr. Simpson, who expects us to know every single*

state in the Union along with all the capitals and state flags. I've only been in school a week, but my head is already crammed full. He says by the end of the year we will know every country and ocean in the world. And he wasn't joking.

Nobody likes him because he is always showing off how smart he is. Being that he just finished high school last spring, he should know more than us kids.

The only good thing he's done so far is to give us all a laugh on the second day of school. It happened when he was waving his pointer at the map and telling us all about San Francisco. Robert Hawkins flicked a spit wad at the side blackboard, and Simpson spun around real quick to try to catch him. His pointer knocked over an ink bottle, which spilled right onto Susie McDougall's lap and ruined her pretty yellow dress. She must be a very unlucky person, because if you recall from the letter I wrote you last winter, she was the one who broke her arm on our hayride. Then Simpson made it worse by trying to daub up the ink with his handkerchief Susie started crying, and he got so flustered that he wiped

his forehead and inked himself all up. We
thought that would slow him down a bit, but
he just keeps piling on the work.

Your brother the scholar,
John

I miss school a lot when I hear stories like that. Maybe I can save up my money and go to college someday. I know Mom would have wanted me to continue my schooling, and a suit-and-tie job would sure beat shoveling in the smoke and the dark.

September 19

For the last week, we've been building our grade alongside a stagecoach line. We're going faster than ever, but every traveler we talk to says the C.P. is doing the same or better.

The race is getting tighter for sure.

October 1
Green River, Wyoming (mile 845)

There is a huge mesa just outside of town called Citadel Rock. The base of it slopes gradually, with shallow gullies trailing away on all sides, but the top half shoots straight up into the sky. The rock looks like a fat knife handle, decorated with alternate stripes of pink and red and brown. I wonder what the view is like from the top? I'll bet I could see all the way back to Chicago.

We're finally into patches of timber again. It feels so good to see some green and have a few hills around to break up the awful flatness.

October 4

As strange as it might sound, I've felt a little closed in the last few days. Though I was itching to get away from that empty desert, I must've gotten used to all the openness without knowing it. Now every time I turn, there's a hill or a tree. Everything seems crowded and squeezed in tight.

October 7

I'm getting over that closed-in feeling. It's strange how a fellow can get used to anything—even a thing like the desert that I hated in the worst way.

★ ★ ★

October 15
Granger, Wyoming

Our tracks crossed the Oregon Trail again today. Pa says that after running north of here along the Sweetwater River and Big Sandy Creek, the trail loops south of our grade. When I asked him why the wagons didn't take a straighter route like the railroad does, he shook his head and said, "Remember the Red Desert?"

It was dumb of me not to figure that one out. Thinking back to the sun-bleached skulls and oxen bones we'd seen on the alkali flats, I realized that anyone with half a brain would rather drive a wagon team fifty miles out of their way than end up dead. Pa says that wagon travel is also easier to the north because the foothills rise more gradually up there.

Even here the Oregon Trail is littered with broken wagon parts and cast-off furniture. I can't begin to imagine everything those wagons have cast aside between here and where they started back in places like Independence, Missouri, which Pa says is nearly a thousand miles away. Every article must have meant a whole lot to someone to tote it this far, and it must have hurt plenty to leave it behind.

This morning, my crew found a wooden grave marker in the middle of the right-of-way. Carved out of a buckboard seat, it was so weathered and gray that it looked fifty years old. But the dates scratched across the top read 1855–1863. The rest of the words, which I could only partly read, said something about OHIO and a girl named SARAH JO.

Dying young has got to be the saddest thing in this whole world. Though it is tough when a grown-up like my mother dies, there is something more cruel in the death of a child. You can't help asking why her and imagining what she might have become.

Between here and Omaha, I've seen hundreds of graves just like that little girl's. They are marked with whatever the families could find at hand—rough boards or sticks or piles of stones—and on even the hottest day, they send a quick chill up my spine.

Our crew was staring at the marker and wondering what to do when Coughlin came along. "Let's get on with it, boys," he said as he wrenched that board out of the dust and tossed it off to the side without even breaking his stride.

When I talked to Pa after supper and told him what a mean thing Coughlin had done, he just shook his head and said, "What's a man going to do?"

Though I know they can't change the survey of this road to steer around a little girl's grave, I wish someone would have at least paused to say a few words to honor her soul. I just pray that those travelers laid her deep enough so she won't be disturbed by all the men and machines.

October 25

Tomorrow we are taking a shot at the tracklaying record. According to the news we get from the papers and from fellows who have traveled this way from Sacramento, it's been a seesaw battle between us and the C.P. all month. We aim to hit her hard at dawn and show them once and for all what we can do. Pa says there are spies working on our line who are getting paid to tell the C.P. just how fast we're moving. I suspect the U.P. is probably doing the same thing.

October 26

Today, I felt like I'd joined the circus. There were photographers and newspaper reporters and a passel of spectators who came from back East (Pa called them "useless fancy folks"). The ladies wore frilly dresses and held parasols to keep off the sun. The fellows were dressed in suits and stovepipe hats. With everyone staring at every move we made, it made me feel like a new animal that had just arrived at the zoo.

A skinny fellow who was puffing on a big cigar tapped

me on the shoulder and asked, "What's your job, sonny?"

I got tongue-tied trying to explain that I was just there to help if I was needed when Pa saved me by saying, "He's my assistant, sir." Then he whispered, "I'm itching to hand those fellows a shovel, Sean, and tell 'em to make themselves useful."

I grinned then, and Bill Flanagan, who had overheard Pa's comment, said, "I wouldn't advise it, Paddy. They'd probably just hurt themselves, or worse, damage good equipment." We had a good laugh at that.

We had breakfast at 4:00 A.M. Getting up that early isn't so bad if you don't have to listen to Jimmy Flynn carry on. Pa had asked me to stand ready to replace anyone who got tuckered out. I doubted that any of the men would need relief, but I was excited to have a chance to watch the show.

I've never seen the fellows work so fast. Before the dust had even settled on the newly set ties, the tenders were clamping their tongs to the rails and rolling them off the beds of the horse carts. And no sooner had the rails clanged down than the spike mauls were ringing out.

I heard a newspaper reporter off to the side reducing the whole tracklaying operation to numbers as he spoke with a lady friend. "Five men to a rail, three blows to a spike, thirty spikes to a rail, four hundred rails to the mile," he said, making it sound as simple as drawing a line across a map.

I guess when you're not doing any real work, you've got the time to count. I hope when he writes his article he mentions that those rails weigh 560 pounds each—that's nearly a quarter of a million pounds of lifting for every single mile we put down.

The teamsters were working their horses so hard bringing the rails forward that they had to hitch fresh animals to their supply carts twice during the morning. The only thing that stalled things a bit was lack of water. Three separate times our tracklaying materials were held up when the locomotives ran dry and overheated. Once an engine lost her steam pressure, and the firebox got so hot that it glowed cherry red. Everyone was afraid she was going to melt down or blow, so some fellows and I helped Ben douse the boiler fire with buckets from his water wagon. But as soon as she cooled down, the firemen filled the reservoir and stoked her back up.

By late afternoon, it was clear that we would set the record, so the fellows wasted a little time laughing and bragging like you would expect. Then, just as they were getting ready to quit, Mac O'Grady teased me. "You want to see if you can bust another maul, boy?" he said.

I stood there not knowing what to say. My face reddened up, and I couldn't decide whether I felt more like cussing him out or running off to hide. Pa and all the spikers were watching as O'Grady pointed the handle of his maul toward me and said, "What do you say?"

I had no choice but to step forward. I set up like Michael Kennedy had shown me last time and bent down to start the spike. When I stood up, my heel caught on the crown of the rail and I almost tripped. The boys behind me chuckled, and I felt my hands turn hot and sweaty.

I swung the maul back and then tried to drop it down smooth like I'd seen the spikers doing all day long. I surprised myself by hitting the spike flush. At that moment, I realized that swinging a pick on the grading crew all those days had improved both my strength and my aim. Why, it was nothing to hit a fat spike head when I'd been nailing tiny cracks and hollows with the sharp end of a pick for days on end.

I hammered the spike flush with my fifth swing, and the rail rang out with a loud *ping*. That was two more strokes than the best spikers take, but I knew I could get better with practice.

A few of the fellows cheered, and even O'Grady let out a "humph" that indicated I'd done a passable job.

Off to the side I heard Mr. Casement, who was standing next to Pa, say, "Looks like we've found ourselves another spiker, Patrick."

When the dust finally settled, we had put down seven and three-fourths miles of rail. "Let those China boys have a crack at *that*," Mac O'Grady said as he swaggered off toward the dining car. Everyone nodded their heads in agreement, and as much as I hate that blowhard, he's probably right. I can't imagine anyone beating our record.

October 27

I just heard that Charlie Crocker, the construction chief of the C.P., has accepted U.P. vice president Durant's $10,000 bet that the C.P. can't beat our single-day record. Crocker said that he wanted to pick the time and the place, and Durant agreed. Crocker claims they'll have a ten-mile day.

All I've got to say is, that's a far piece to walk in a day's time, much less lay rails.

Pa laughed when he heard about the bet. "Crocker can't boil enough tea to keep those Chinamen going that long," he said.

I don't know how Pa can have so many strong opinions about the Chinese, being that the only Chinese he knows are a family named Pan who run a laundry back in Chicago.

★ ★ ★

October 29

I'm not a spiker yet — that would have been way too much to ask — but I am working as a rail tender. I can see why Pa started me off as a water carrier. Heaving these 560-pound rails around is a heck of a lot harder than lifting water buckets. And I thought that was tough work when I first got out here.

V.P. Durant has been hovering around all the crews. He's asking questions and giving orders all the time. Today, I heard him tell General Casement that if we can average two miles of track per day, we should be able to do three.

I'll bet that fellow doesn't know how to do much more than carry his money bags to the bank.

November 3

Casement hasn't paid us for two weeks. Pa says the blowhards from back East like Durant have fouled up the finances of the U.P. so bad that the railroad is short of cash. Whatever the reason, the men are getting more ornery every day.

November 11

I heard about a town just up ahead called Bear River City, which is even wilder than Julesburg. Bill says that the citizens have formed a committee to cut back on the violence. Yesterday, they hung a gunman named Little Jack O'Neil and two of his buddies.

Executing people without a fair trial seems like a strange way to stop violence.

November 14

Working as an iron man—loading rails and rolling them off the cart—is a tricky business. It takes perfect timing for the four of us to clamp our tongs on a rail and drop it in place. If I lift late, the fellows give me a good cussing, and if I lift too early, I risk ripping my back.

But the most important thing is to watch your feet. When they sing out, "Down," that rail is going down whether you're ready or not, and you better get your boots clear. A rail tender named Peter McKinney got his toes caught under a rail last week and he yowled like a gut-shot coyote. No one blamed him for yelling, either, because 560 pounds of iron can mash up a foot so bad that you can't hardly recognize it.

November 16

Mac O'Grady finally got what he deserved today. He was picking on the younger fellows like he always does, teasing and calling them names. But no one paid him any mind until he started in on Peter McKinney.

Poor McKinney was just getting so he could limp around in an oversized boot that was padded with bandages, and he was anxious to help the tracklayers. He said he needed to get back on the payroll so he could send money to his wife and eight kids in St. Louis. He was doing all he could—opening spike kegs, handing the fellows their mauls, and the like. That's when O'Grady walked over and set the head of his spike maul right on top of McKinney's bad foot.

"The weather's gettin' a bit cool, ain't it, Pete?" he said, leaning on the handle of his maul to see how much pressure McKinney could stand.

That's when Pa stepped in. "Leave him be, Mac," Pa said.

"Mind your own business, Paddy," he said. "You ain't his mother."

Pa walked right over without another word and grabbed that spike maul out of O'Grady's hand and tossed it down.

You could see the relief on McKinney's face when the pressure eased, and I thought that would be the end of it. But O'Grady was piping mad. He shoved Pa back and took a swing. I opened my mouth to warn Pa, but he'd already seen the fist coming and blocked it with his left hand. Then, instead of punching O'Grady like you'd expect, he gave him a quick backhand, and then another. His hands flashed out so quick, they were a blur—right, left, right. O'Grady's head snapped back each time.

I could see that O'Grady was knocked out on his feet, so I yelled, "Stop, Pa," and caught him by the shoulder. Pa whirled with a wild-eyed look, and for an instant I thought he might take a swing at me. Then he was back to himself and apologizing for losing control. O'Grady woke up a bit later, covered with dust, but no worse for wear.

Tonight, when I opened my journal, I realized where Pa's anger came from. Today would have been his anniversary again. If only someone had warned Mac O'Grady to be better behaved for just one day.

November 18

The last two days, Mac O'Grady has been so polite that I don't hardly recognize him.

★ ★ ★

November 19
Bear River City, Wyoming

All hell broke loose yesterday. Pardon my swearing, but what happened over in Bear River City today made the fight between Pa and Mac O'Grady look like a ladies' tea party.

Bear Town, as the locals call the place, had sprung up just beyond the end of the track. The gamblers and fancy ladies and saloon keepers had set up shop, but for a change, they weren't the cause of the trouble.

The fellows who started it all are two brothers named Leigh and Richmond Freeman. They've been following us road builders for a long while, toting a one-ton printing press (which the U.P. carried for free on its train) and publishing a newspaper called the *Frontier Index*. A lot of the fellows have been riled up about the things they've put in their paper lately criticizing the U.P. Ben gets especially sad when he hears what the Freemans have spouted off about Negroes being subhuman and not deserving their freedom. In a way, I'm almost glad that Ben can't read—the stuff in the Freemans' paper is that ugly.

Well, this time the Freemans went overboard. They printed an editorial saying that Ulysses S. Grant was "a whiskey-bloated, squaw-ravishing adulterer" and a "nigger worshipping mogul." I don't know what a "mogul" is, and I don't think most of the other U.P. men do, either, but we all know what the rest means. Since a good portion of our men served under Grant during the war, they didn't take kindly to such insults.

However, what really put them over the edge was the evil things that those Freemans wrote about President Lincoln. Not only did they call Lincoln "filthy" and "lecherous," but they went so far as to say that John Wilkes Booth did a good deed by assassinating him.

As mean-spirited as those words were, if the men had stayed sober and if they'd been paid on time, everything might have turned out okay. But Casement is a full month behind on our wages now, and once the men got liquored up, there was no stopping them.

When the trouble started, Pa and I were walking past a little board-and-batten shack that called itself the R. R. House restaurant. I heard some yelling and looked up the street. There must have been two hundred fellows headed toward the Freemans' office. They were a fearsome sight, swinging ax handles and spike mauls and yelling at people to clear out of their way.

Even though I wanted to follow along and see what happened, Pa got me out of there quick. A few minutes later, I was glad he did. We weren't halfway back to the work train when I heard the first shots. They were just a couple of flat cracks that sounded like a Colt .44.

I didn't think much of it because gunfire isn't unusual in a frontier town. Then, all of a sudden, it sounded like a whole army was letting loose. Six-shooters and shotguns and rifles were popping off so fast that it could have been a Gatling gun.

"Good Lord," Pa whispered, and shook his head. I think all the shooting reminded him of the war, because he turned as pale as I'd ever seen him.

November 20

I found out where the shooting came from. According to Bill Flanagan, who took a slug in the forearm and looks like he'll be laid up for a while, the U.P. men stormed into the Freemans' office and smashed it up. But when they stepped back out into the street, a bunch of town vigilantes opened up on them. Twenty-five men were killed. Dozens more were wounded.

The sad thing is that the U.P. just dug a big hole and buried all those fellows together. No service. No markers. No nothing.

Pa said that the railroad wanted to keep it quiet. Two fellows who they didn't hush up were those snakes the Freemans. Somebody tipped them off before the U.P. men got to their office, and they sneaked off like the cowards they are.

I can't believe that the railroad expects to get away with piling a bunch of shot-up bodies into an open grave. Those men were pounding spikes and slurping down coffee yesterday, yet today it's like they were never alive. One of them—Charlie O'Farrell—was the finest clog dancer and singer that I've ever seen. His voice was so pure that he could make me smile by just saying, "Top of the morning, Sean." I know for a fact that he's got a girl back in Kerry, Ireland, and he was saving up money to send for her. Are we supposed to pretend that he just disappeared?

I tried to write this all in a letter to John, but it was hard to find words to describe the sadness and anger I'm feeling. I know if Indians had killed those fellows, every newspaper in this country would be scrambling to print the story with a fat headline. There would've been a heap of bad news then.

November 23

I've been checking the papers every chance I get, and the U.P. must be doing a good job of covering things up, because there is barely a word about what they are calling "the Bear River riot."

Mr. Casement decided to teach the Bear River City people a lesson. Instead of building a siding—a branch of the track—into town like the U.P. usually does, we laid our tracks straight on by. Those local businessmen are probably upset, but they should have thought a bit more before they shot up our men.

November 26

I celebrated my second Thanksgiving on the railroad today. It sure was nice of President Lincoln to start this holiday back up again. We got part of the afternoon off, and the cooks gave us an extra-nice meal with biscuits and real gravy instead of just pot drippings. Pa took me to a pie shop that a lady has set up in a tent, and I got a big piece of pumpkin pie. Though the crust was a bit chewy, I'm not about to complain.

I wrote Aunt Katie a letter and told her how much I miss her and her lemon-cream pies.

November 28
Aspen Station, Wyoming (mile 937)

I can see why they call this place Aspen. The hills are covered with solid stands of aspen trees. Last month there must have been golden leaves rippling all over these slopes, but now everything has gone gray. The trunks and branches are just bare sticks poking up into the sky. Back home our oaks hold on to their leaves well into the winter and leave us with a splash of color to remember summer by. If there weren't a few evergreens to break up the grayness of these mountains, this wouldn't look much better than the desert country we left behind.

Just east of town — between here and a place called Piedmont — we crossed the Oregon Trail for what Pa says will be the last time. In the short, rutted stretch of road that I could see, I counted two graves, a broken wagon wheel, a discarded chest of drawers, and a brand-new baby's cradle.

December 4
Evanston, Wyoming (mile 955)

The weather is turning colder every day. Though it was ugly working in the Dale Creek Gorge last winter, at least it was sheltered. Here, the wind hits you from all sides.

We've been back in the bunk car for a week now, and the fellow who sleeps across from us has been coughing all night and keeping everyone awake.

They've shipped in a newfangled steam shovel to work in the rougher cuts. When that machine is digging, you can feel the earth shake a hundred yards away. The chains and pulleys make a terrible racket, but it's amazing how much dirt it can move. The bucket is bigger than three good-sized men. Yesterday, a half-dozen fellows posed for a picture, standing out on the boom of that steam shovel. I kept thinking, what if those gears slip? But they just set their hands on their hips and stared straight at the camera, looking as if they didn't have a care in the world.

If the U.P. gets many more fancy machines, they won't need any more pick-and-shovel men. Pa says they've ordered a steam-driven pile driver, too. Maybe they'll even build a machine to pound spikes some day.

December 5

Everyone is hoping for an open winter, but it is already snowing hard enough to hold up the trains. The mail is so slow that it takes us two or three weeks to get a letter from Chicago.

Utah

December 10
Wasatch Town, Utah (mile 966)

The ground is frozen so hard that we have to set off powder charges to move every shovelful of dirt. We should have quit for the winter long ago, but rumors say that the C.P. is still racing right along, and we have to keep up.

Whether we are loading rails on the carts or dropping them in place for the spikers, we have to be careful of our footing. It would be easy to tip a load of iron over on a man in this weather. It's worse, too, because the animals get skittish in the snow.

Sometimes my fingers get so stiff and cold from hanging on to the rail tongs that I can't even straighten them out when quitting time comes. The boys I really feel sorry for, though, are the ones who ride as scouts and couriers. I watched an army scout come into the Wasatch Depot this evening who was frosted up so bad that he looked like he was frozen right to his saddle. His horse didn't seem very happy, either.

December 16

The trains are finally running again, but with the kind of weather we've been having, who knows how long the line will stay open?

That fancy new steam shovel has frozen up. I can't say I'm surprised.

December 24

Pa was going to take me to the Wasatch Hotel for Christmas Eve dinner today, but it was so cold in the lobby that we could see our breath. The manager tried to convince us to stay, but we went down the street to a little dining hall instead. Though the only thing on the menu was steak and potatoes, at least it was warm inside. They claimed the meat was beefsteak, but it was so stringy and gamy tasting that Pa figured it was bull elk. Even if our food took some extra chewing, I enjoyed getting away from the stink of that work train. No one has taken a bath since the weather turned cold.

December 25

Christmas on the Wasatch Range. It's hard being so far from home on a holiday. Pa did his best to try to make it seem like a real Christmas, but it isn't the same without the rest of the family. Though John and I scrapped sometimes, I miss him and my aunt and uncle more and more lately.

For a present, Pa got me some copies of a magazine called *Student and Schoolmate*. It's got adventure stories in it about a character named Ragged Dick. They're easy reading, and the author has a funny name — Oliver Optic. I wonder if that is his real name. When I first started on the railroad, the fellows were passing around a story called "The Celebrated Jumping Frog of Calaveras County," by Mr. Mark Twain. I thought that was his real name until I read in the paper that he is actually Samuel Clemens.

I gave Pa a fine ivory-handled clasp knife that I bought in C. S. Watson's store. I know that I paid too much, but it's hard to find nice things out here. I also sent a knife home to John. I sure hope he doesn't cut himself, as I would hear about that from Aunt Katie.

The weather has been gray and gloomy through most of December. Sometimes a fog settles in over the mountains and doesn't lift for a week. Snow has piled up as high as the windows of the trains, and traffic has slowed to a crawl. They say that a train over in Evans Pass is completely stalled, and that the tracks are blocked all the way back to the Red Desert and Rawlins.

Pa says that the C.P. played it a lot smarter in the mountains. They built miles and miles of snowsheds over their tracks in the high passes, giving them smooth sailing compared to us.

★ ★ ★

December 26

There was an accident in Echo Canyon today. The construction train was creeping down the grade like it has to when the rails are slick. Pa and I were riding on the flatcar at the end of the train when someone shouted, "Runaway!"

I looked up the hill and saw four loaded flatcars hurtling toward us. It's funny when cars uncouple on flat stretches. A little slack in the linkage is all it takes, and the coupling pin can fall out. Then the fellows have a good chuckle as the engine chugs, leaving half of the train behind.

But cars getting away on a steep grade are serious business. The fellow who'd lost the cars at the top whistled, and our engineer thought fast. He opened up his throttle and lay on his whistle to clear the tracks. Though we picked up speed, I could see the cars were closing fast. Pa and I both got up to jump clear, but the trestle at the bottom of the canyon was getting so close that he shook his head and pulled me back down.

All we could do was hunker down tight and watch those tons of iron flying toward us. We hit that trestle full steam ahead, and the engineer kept blasting his whistle all the way across. The sound just about split my eardrums as it echoed up and down the rock cut and mixed in with the clatter of the wheels and the creaking of the bridge timbers.

When we hit the flat on the far side of the bridge, the cars were closing so fast that it looked like we were goners. Then I noticed the loose ties on the end of our flatcar and yelled, "We can derail her."

Pa must've thought I was talking about derailing our own train, but then he realized that I meant we might be able to knock the oncoming cars off the track. We each slid a tie off the back of our flatcar. As the ties hit between the rails, they flipped over once and then rolled sideways. For a minute, I thought the flatcar was just going to knock the ties out of the way, but the left wheel suddenly hopped up in the air like we'd hoped.

What we didn't expect was the sudden increase in speed. That airborne car shot straight toward us. I grabbed for Pa's arm, wondering if it was too late to jump. But as suddenly as the flatcar rose, it fell. With a terrible grinding sound, the wheel crashed down between the rails. The rear cars jackknifed and tipped on their sides, skidding to a halt in a mess of wood and iron.

You'd think they would have congratulated me and Pa on saving the work train and given us a day off with pay. Instead, we had to shovel and pry through that wreckage until way past supper time, clearing the line for traffic.

December 28
Echo Summit, Utah (mile 969)

As another Christmas present, Pa has promoted me to the spiking crew. He said that Mr. Casement heard about my fast thinking on the back of the flatcar and told him that he should've made me a spiker long ago.

The fellows are always skeptical about trying to fit in a new man, but they were open-minded enough to give me a chance. Though it usually takes me four or five hits to get a spike down, I'm proud to say that I haven't broken a single maul yet.

One thing I don't have to worry about is Mac O'Grady's teasing. Ever since Pa put him in his place, he's been especially polite around Peter McKinney and me.

As bitter cold and snowy as it is, we still haven't quit laying track. The second big tunnel project is under way near the summit, and it's going slow. The rock is a whole lot tougher here than it was back at St. Mary's. Bill Flanagan says they are trying out a blasting oil called "nitroglycerin."

December 29
Castle Rock, Utah (mile 975)

There is a curious rock formation above the river called Castle Rock. The name fits perfectly, because it must be three hundred feet high and has squarish sides that give it the look of a fortress. One little knob on top could almost pass for a watchtower. I don't doubt that the whole court of Camelot would fit on that rock. Why, if it wasn't so wintry; I could almost imagine Sir Galahad or Sir Lancelot riding down to greet us.

In spite of the constant weather delays, we are making some progress with the track.

December 30

After envying the spikers all these months, it is exciting to finally be a part of their crew. I love the heft of my hickory-handled maul and the ring of the steel.

The one thing that is hard to get used to is swinging with the same motion all day long. On the grading crew there was more variety. I'd switch off between picking and shoveling, and hauling fill, but on this crew it's pound, pound all day long.

It is satisfying to hit those spikes home, though. And I stay so busy that I don't even mind the cold. *Ping, ping, ping.* The sound rings out. *Ping, ping, ping.* The spike bites into the wood, and I step forward again.

I don't always finish in three hits, but I keep trying. Pa claims I need to swing smoother and just let the weight of my maul do the work, but I love to let loose with all my strength. That's when I usually clang the rail, and everyone but Pa has a good chuckle. While the fellows tease me about my poor aim, he stands off by himself and shakes his head.

All I can do is try my best, and spiking down these rails gives me the feeling that I'm playing a direct part in tying this country together. To prove it, I only have to glance back and see those new rails pointing all the way back to Omaha.

January 3, 1869

Everyone is talking about nitroglycerin. Since the tunnels are going so slow, Durant has ordered the crews to use it full-time. The powder men say it is so dangerous that it should be banned.

A few of the fellows started telling stories about nitro after supper tonight. We'd all heard about the Wells Fargo office in San Francisco, where a shipment of the stuff exploded not too long ago. Fourteen people were killed, and witnesses said that an arm flew out a third-story window. But a man named Kelly told us a story I'd never heard. Kelly used to live in New York, and he said that a box of the stuff went off by accident in a place called Greenwich Village. A friend of his, who was a porter in the Wyoming Hotel, smelled something hot one morning. He found a case of nitro, smoking and bubbling in a cloak room. When he tossed it out into the street, the blast blew away half the housefronts on the block and left a huge hole of boiling yellow mud in the middle of the street. Kelly says that his buddy is still stone deaf.

Another fellow told us about a ship down in Panama that was unloading a crate of nitro a couple of years back. The cargo net accidentally bumped the side of the boat, and the steamship and the pier both disappeared in a huge ball of flame.

When another man laughed and said that nothing could be that powerful, he looked him right in the eye and said, "Sixty men died. I was a longshoreman and saw it with my own eyes. Charred wood and hunks of flesh landed on tin roofs a half a mile away."

There was no bragging in his voice, just a quiet sadness that told me he was telling the gospel truth. I hope I never have to fool with that stuff.

January 5

It's usually tough to get old-timers to agree, but every single one of them says that this is the worst winter in the history of the Wasatch Range. I sure wouldn't argue.

January 8

Though Pa is not one to complain, he's upset about the shoddy work that they are having us do on the track. He says the grades are too steep and the curves are too sharp for safe travel. But whenever he talks to Mr. Casement about it, Casement says Durant is the one who's pushing.

"Every mile is money in his pocket," Pa said today. "But what good is track that can't hold up a train?"

January 15
Echo City, Utah (mile 991)

Outside of Echo City are two high cliffs on opposite sides of our roadway. I heard Michael Kennedy call one of the cliffs "Death Rock," and I asked him why. He said that during the Mormon War, a militiaman taunted a soldier who was standing on the opposite ridge to take a shot at him. Though he was more than a quarter of a mile away, the bullet caught him flush in the head.

Along with the tents and shanties here in Echo City, a few wood-frame storefronts have gone up. There's a Wells Fargo office, Watson Hardware, Asplund and Conner Dining Hall, a bank, and a furnishing goods store, in addition to the usual mix of saloons and hotels.

January 16

We are spending as much time fixing derailments as laying track. Nothing is worse than trying to jack a heavy locomotive back onto the rails when it's this cold. Half the time, I've got no feeling in my fingers. I skinned my knuckles so bad yesterday that the back of my hand got crusted up with blood and stuck inside my glove, but I was so cold that I never felt a thing.

I swear a fellow could cut his fingers plumb off in this weather and hardly know it.

January 17

We are finally done for the winter. Durant was hoping to make it an even thousand miles before we quit, but we came up a few rails short.

January 18

Storms howl through the Wasatch nearly every day. Some nights the wind hits such a high pitch that I have to cover my ears to get to sleep. The walls and ceiling of the bunk car are thick with frost every morning. I miss the warm weather and that little tent we used to pitch beside the grade.

Winter out here is nothing but shoveling. Back in Chicago, it meant skating and sliding games and sleigh rides. One day, when John and I were little, Mother helped us make a snowman that was the spitting image of our uncle Willy. We dressed him in an old coat, put a hat on his head backwards, and stuck a big cigar in his mouth. When Willy came home from work, half the neighborhood was gathered in our yard having a good laugh.

January 20

Though the tracklaying has stopped, the tunnel work is going full speed ahead. As dangerous as the nitro is, Pa says the crews are blasting away six feet of rock a day instead of the two they made with black powder.

One of the most dangerous things about the nitro is disposing of the used blasting cans. Even a half a drop left in those containers can explode without warning. Two fellows got cut up bad last week when they tossed an empty can into a gully and it blew. Now they're taking the empties away from camp to dispose of them. The boys pile up the cans, start a little fire, and then run for cover. The last time they blew up some cans, Pa and I could see tin shrapnel sparkling in the sky from a half mile away.

Since John loves fireworks, I wrote and told him about how loud those blasts are, but I didn't mention how bad they startle Pa. Last Tuesday, when we were walking toward the dining car and a pile of cans went up, Pa ducked his head like he was ready to dive for cover. He's embarrassed whenever he jumps like that, but I can't blame him for not being able to forget the war.

February 16 (1,000 miles)

We reached the one-thousand-mile marker today. It's a lone pine tree that looks like it was planted beside the tracks for the sole purpose of showing how much track we have laid from Omaha. It has a sign tied on its lower branches that reads 1,000-MILE TREE, and I'll bet that every excursionist who comes this way is going to want to stop here and have their picture taken.

Snow again, but I'm hoping it'll just be flurries.

February 18

The snow is still coming down hard, and the wind has picked up. Just when I figured that winter was done, it's time to start shoveling again.

★ ★ ★

February 19

The snow is ten feet deep on the level stretches of track, and it's drifted twice that bad on the slopes. It took one hundred of us shoveling for ten hours to clear a rock cut. Then the wind came up again and closed it back up in only an hour.

I felt like heaving my shovel down the mountain and walking back to Chicago.

February 23

As tough as the blizzard was out here, they say it's worse in the Black Hills. The drifts are forty feet deep in places — that's high enough to cover the telegraph poles over twice. General Casement told Pa that it may be three weeks before the rail line between Laramie and Rawlins is open, and he's worried about getting enough supplies for the upcoming season.

February 29
Devil's Gate, Utah (mile 1,018)

The tracklaying for 1869 has already started. Pa says that Durant is pushing harder than ever, and he doesn't care a lick about the quality of the work. He wants his miles.

Spring is finally creeping up on us. Snow melt is rushing down every creek and canyon.

We reached a bridge that spans a black chasm called Devil's Gate. As scary as the Dale Creek Bridge was, Devil's Gate beats it hands down. The bridge is anchored with the same sort of feeble ropes and cabling, but what makes it so frightening is the river. Dark, foam-flecked water roars past the pilings and makes the whole framework of the bridge tremble.

Our engineer pushed the work train over the trestle one car at a time. The tracks creaked and swayed. When I looked down from the flatcar, I could see that most of the timbering was just green logs with ragged strips of bark hanging loose in the wind.

When it comes time to head home, I just may shop for a steamship ticket if they haven't shored up this bridge.

March 1

A blacksmith did a dumb thing this afternoon when he was showing off for the mule skinners. He put a drop of nitro on his anvil and hit it with a horseshoe hammer. The hammer kicked back and broke his jaw. Lucky no one else got hurt.

March 4

We've had our first big thaw, and it's turned this whole place into a mud hole. The ground under the ties is so spongy that the trains can't go any faster than five miles per hour.

In the soft places, the ties are pounded down into the slush so far that you get a shower when the trains go by. If you don't stand clear, water and muck shoots right up in your face. As soon as the train is gone, the ties pop back up, and the water and mud gurgle down around them.

In the worst places, the packed snow has melted completely away under the ties and left the rails hanging way up in the air. The locomotive engineers are shaking their heads all the time. I'm afraid there's bound to be an accident soon.

March 6

My spiking is getting better all the time, but I've still got to fight the urge to overswing. Pa has told me again and again to let the maul do the work and to not worry if I can't put every spike down in three hits.

I don't always listen, though, because I love to swing hard. If my rhythm is good, and I'm knocking the spikes down in four blows, I can't help but try to do it in three.

That's when I foul up and ding the rail or send a spike flying down the tracks.

Pa bites his lower lip then, and mumbles, "Take her easy, son," and I know he'll be talking to me after supper. My worst fear is that I'll mess up so bad that he'll send me back to work with that pig, Jimmy Flynn.

March 7
Ogden, Utah (mile 1,028)

Though the Mormons may be serious people who dress in plain clothing, they sure know how to celebrate the arrival of a railroad. As we laid the rails into town, a brass band led a parade of people down Main Street to greet us. The locomotives blew their whistles all at once, and a squad of soldiers answered with an artillery salute.

They also hung a big banner between two arching trees that read, HAIL TO THE HIGHWAY OF NATIONS! UTAH BIDS YOU WELCOME! I finally got to see Brigham Young, the head Mormon. I couldn't help but wonder if a man who had that many wives might look different from an average fellow, but I didn't notice anything exceptional about him. His hat sat low on his forehead, giving him a broad-faced look. He shaves his mustache but has a chin full of black-and-silver whiskers. As ordinary as he looked, when he started his welcoming speech, you could tell by the way everyone in the crowd nodded their heads that he is the boss in these parts. Several U.P. officials also spoke. Their speeches were so boring that I was really glad when the last fellow stepped down from the podium.

After the ceremony was over, Pa and I explored the town. Ogden has a more orderly and settled look to it than most of the railroad towns. Though the streets are a series of mud puddles, like every place on the frontier, the storefronts are mainly wood and look permanent compared to the raggedy tents I've seen so far. The amazing thing is that there aren't any saloons. I heard a lot of grumbling from the boys when they saw there were no taverns, but if you ask me, I'd sure rather live in a clean place like this than any of the towns back along the line. It would be nice to walk down a street at night without having to get past fancy ladies swinging derringers from their dress pockets and liquored-up fellows who are ready to empty their six-shooters at the drop of a hat.

A storekeeper told us that Salt Lake City, the Utah territorial capital, which is located just south of here, is so pretty that it puts even Ogden to shame. And everyone says that Brigham Young's home is as big as a hotel. No wonder, with all those wives.

★ ★ ★

March 8

As the weather warms, I like my job as a spiker more
and more. The pace is so hectic that I barely have time
to catch my breath, but there is something in the rhythm
of the work that makes the days fly. I am learning to
be more patient, too. If I run into an extra-hard tie that
takes a few extra swings, I fight the urge to overswing. It
seems like the only time I mess up is when Pa is looking.
Maybe I'm trying too hard to impress him.

I feel like I've come a long way from my water-
carrying and snake-hunting days. When things are going
well, I wish that my mother were still alive to see me.

I got a letter from John today.

Dear Sean,
*   The wind has really been roaring lately.*
We've had a three-day blowout of the northeast.
The waves are crashing so hard down on the
shore that I can hear them in my bedroom, even
with the windows closed.
*   Donald Reily dropped out of school last week*
to go to work in his father's livery stable and
funeral parlor: I don't think I'd care to spend my
life shoveling manure and fitting dead people for
pine boxes, but some days even that would be
an improvement over school. Don's the third boy

in my class to go to work full-time this spring.
Sometimes I think about looking for a job myself,
but we both know how Mother felt about us
learning as much as we could. Aunt Katie is
dead set against me quitting school, too.

You mentioned in your last letter that you
are thinking about finishing high school some
day and maybe even going on to college. Maybe
you can become a lawyer and get me a job
downtown. Mr. Simpson has been talking so
much about exports and imports lately that
I am about ready to emigrate — that means
to leave the country you are living in and go
somewhere else.

Meanwhile, I'll keep on studying.

Your favorite geographer,
John

March 9

As if enough people aren't getting injured by acci-
dents on this railroad, I'm ashamed to say that some
of the Irish workers have been hurting the Chinese on
purpose. With the U.P. and the C.P. working so close
together these days, the blasting is twice as dangerous.
The Chinese always wave to let us know when they are

about to set off a charge so we can clear out of the way. But, for some reason, we don't warn them. Yesterday, one of our grading crews set off a charge that killed three Chinese workers and injured a half dozen more.

Then Bill Flanagan and his buddies had the gall to laugh about it during dinner!

March 10

Of all the foolish waste I have seen so far, the Big Trestle wins the prize. The construction crews of the C.P. and U.P. are working side by side to build their tracks over a deep gully called Spring Creek Ravine. C.P. workers have been hauling material for the last three months, filling in a hole 500 feet long by 170 feet deep that they call the Big Fill.

The foolish part comes in when the U.P. decided to build a bridge instead. So even though the C.P. is nearly done with their project, the U.P. has decided to span the very same gorge with a trestle running parallel to the C.P. grade. I'm sure they are hoping the government will pay both railroads for doing the same work.

People complain about bank robbers and railroad bandits, but to my mind, the owners of these rail lines are the lowest sort of thieves. They are squeezing every dollar they can from the government. Call it a contract or a subsidy or whatever name you like, I say it is stealing, pure and simple.

March 11

Whenever they get the chance, the Irish fellows hoot and holler at the Chinese workers. They call them "godless heathens" and make fun of how they dress and how they look and how short they are. I'm ashamed to say that my pa joins right in with the teasing. For the life of me, I can't understand why they have it in for these folks.

March 12

I may have figured out why the Irish resent the Chinese so much. I think the Irish may be jealous of all the work the Chinese get done. Though our fellows make a lot of noise, I really think the Chinese accomplish more. While we were waiting for the rails to be brought forward today, I watched the C.P. crew filling a ravine today. At first I thought they were moving at a snail's pace. But the more I watched, the more I realized that it wasn't slow, it was just smooth and steady. Looking at them, I can see what Pa means about keeping an even pace when you work.

They have two-wheeled dump carts for moving the

fill, and they never stop rolling. As three carts are being dumped into the ravine, three more are being shoveled full. Their draft animals plod along at the same pace as the workers, and they never seem to need any lashing or prodding. If they are short of mules or horses, men don't hesitate to pull the carts themselves. Yet as hard as they work, they manage to stay neat and clean compared to our fellows.

In the place of a water carrier, they hire a boy who brings tea out to the men. Across his shoulders, he balances a pole hung with two used powder kegs filled with warm tea. At the work site he dumps the tea into a forty-gallon whiskey barrel that's fixed with a little spigot for the men to tap their own drinks.

Since our water gets awful green and scummy at times, it would make sense for us to drink tea, too, or at least boil our water. Instead, our fellows suffer through their stomachaches and diarrhea and laugh at what Flanagan calls the "weak-kneed tea sops." It don't make any sense to me.

March 13

Another Chinese worker died in a blasting "accident" today. I swear, if Bill Flanagan makes one more joke about "burying rice eaters under rock piles where they belong," I will go after him with a pick handle.

I heard that President Grant is getting ready to settle where the rails will meet. If he talks to all the bosses, I wish he would tell them to stop blowing up innocent people.

March 14

Though General Casement is usually all business, I was surprised to see him humming and smiling this afternoon. When I asked Pa why the general was so happy, he said that the U.P. board of directors just voted to cut back on Durant's authority.

It will be good to have that fellow out of our hair. I wish they would kick him out altogether.

March 24

It finally happened. The Chinese decided that they'd had enough, and they planted a grave—that's a charge that's meant to kill—above a rock cut where a U.P. gang was working. The blast killed one Irishman, and injured three others.

Suddenly our fellows have agreed to call a truce. They promise to give fair warning of all our blasting from now on if the Chinese will do the same. My question is, why does it take someone dying to knock some sense into our heads?

March 25

They had a bad derailment back at Echo yesterday. A boxcar loaded with passengers jumped off the tracks on a tight curve and came within inches of sliding into a deep ravine. Pa says it's dumb luck that a passel of people haven't died in a wreck yet.

March 27
Corinne, Utah (mile 1,055)

The payroll is up to date again, and just in time. Another town has sprung to life at the end of the track, and this one is as lively as they get. All the desperadoes and gamblers who weren't welcome in Ogden have settled here. Fellows who have been itching to celebrate all month finally have a place to go. (Pa thinks General Casement had to take the money out of his own pocket to pay the men because the U.P. is in such bad trouble.)

The Mormons are staying clear of Corinne.

★ ★ ★

April 7

The C.P.'s tracks are only fifty miles west of us now.

April 8

I can't believe the greed of these two railroads. It looked like we would be joining the rails together in just a few days, but since both companies are paid by the mile, they keep preparing two separate grades side by side. I swear, if the government doesn't tell them to stop, these rascals will build two sets of tracks all the way from Omaha to Sacramento.

April 9

As fast as everyone has been rushing lately, it's no surprise that there's been an accident. This afternoon a man on the grading crew was tamping some powder into a drill hole with a steel lining bar. He accidentally struck a rock and set off a spark. Ben, who had his wagon parked nearby, said the explosion blew the poor fellow a hundred feet in the air, and that he broke every bone in his body when he landed. Three men who were standing nearby were cut up by stone fragments and burned badly.

April 10

President Ulysses S. Grant ordered officials of both the U.P. and the C.P. to meet and settle this craziness about where these railroads are going to join. After some haggling, they agreed on Promontory, Utah Territory.

When the president had all those crooks in one room, he should have had them hauled off to jail.

April 12

Today would have been Mother's thirty-fifth birthday. Pa was real quiet after dinner. I thought about mentioning her birthday, but Pa didn't seem to be in a talking mood. So I just let it rest, and for once, Bill Flanagan took the hint and was quiet, too.

Though I know Pa will never get over it — and neither will John nor I — he is showing more strength all the time.

April 18

I've been thinking a lot lately about what I aim to do when this job is done. General Casement can already see the end of things, and he's letting a few more men go each day.

Pa says there will be lots of jobs on a new rail line

they are planning to build from Duluth to Seattle called the Northern Pacific.

Would I be foolish enough to put myself through this all over again? Whatever we decide, our first stop will be Chicago. I never thought I could miss that city so much. After I visit with my family, the first thing I want to do is stroll up Michigan Avenue and watch the boats offshore and look in the shopwindows and do absolutely nothing until it is time to sit down to dinner.

April 22

Word is that the crew chief of the C.P., Charlie Crocker, is finally going to take Durant up on his ten-thousand-dollar tracklaying bet. No one knows why he's taken this long to give it a try, but it's supposed to happen any day now.

The fellows are laughing over the bet. "What's Crocker going to do with all his little Chinamen—give them toy rails to play with?" Bill Flanagan declared over supper.

Though I don't admire his bragging, I've got to believe that no one will ever match the seven and three-fourths miles we laid last October.

★ ★ ★

April 28

The C.P. tried to beat our all-time tracklaying record today. Mr. Casement asked Pa to come along as a witness, and since the tracklaying has slowed on our side—why rush when we can't go any farther than Promontory?—he brought me along to watch.

I was impressed with how organized things were. The C.P. track boss, James Strobridge, had his materials ready, and a crew of five thousand, including iron men, spikers, tampers, and mule skinners, were lined up before daybreak.

Strobridge is so valuable to the C.P. that they've coupled a personal car to their work train for his family. His wife, Hannah, and her six kids travel right along with him. She's hung potted plants across the front of the car to make it into a real homey place, and she even keeps a singing canary in a cage outside her door.

A whistle blew at dawn, and with a huge clang of iron a crew of Chinese fellows unloaded the first sixteen cars of rails. Though they looked mighty skinny, they had their handcars piled with rails in only minutes. Then they flew down the grade, dumping rails, spikes, and fishplates within easy reach of the all-Irish crew of iron men.

As quick as a man could walk, the rails were set, bolted, and spiked. Each worker did his job so smoothly that it looked like the opening night of a well-rehearsed play.

Shortly after they started laying the track, Pa pulled out his watch to time their progress. He was astonished to see that they had put down two hundred feet of rail in a single minute. "They'll never keep it up," he muttered.

By 6:00 A.M. the C.P. had spiked and tamped an amazing two miles of track. Mr. Casement, who paced alongside the completed section, could do nothing but admit that the work was well done.

Their planning was so perfect that I could tell right then that no locomotives would be running dry, like they did on our record day, and no one would be slowed by a lack of materials. They had things figured to the last keg of spikes.

Through the morning the newspapermen jotted down notes and counted the tons of iron. By lunchtime the C.P. had done six solid miles of track, and I knew that barring a disaster, there would be no stopping them.

Though the C.P.'s Chinese men had been working side by side with the Irish, as soon as the lunch whistle blew, it was like someone had drawn a line in the sand between the two groups. I overheard a reporter ask through an interpreter why the Chinese ate by themselves. A man who looked to be the leader of his crew said that it was their wish. He explained that they hired their own cooks and shipped most of their food in from China. They ate things I'd never heard of, like dried cuttlefish and abalone and bamboo sprouts and seaweed. Maybe that food helps those Chinese work as hard as they do.

The minute lunch was over, the crews melted back together and hit her as hard as ever. When dusk fell, by our engineer's own measurement they'd finished exactly ten miles and fifty-six feet of track. To test the quality of the work, Crocker ordered his heaviest locomotive to take a forty-mile-per-hour run down the full length of the track. I was impressed that hardly a tie trembled.

The newspaper reporters figured that the C.P. iron crew had lifted well over two million pounds of iron by the end of the day. I heard those iron men got four days' wages for their work. That comes to six or seven dollars per man, which sounds pretty good until you compare it to the $10,000 that Crocker won.

April 29

Today we figured out why Crocker took so long to take up Durant on his bet. That old fox waited until we were closer than ten miles to Promontory, knowing there would be no way we could match his record.

★ ★ ★

April 30

I saw a line of naked Chinamen tonight. Actually, they weren't all naked at once; they were just taking turns, walking up to a big tub of water, dropping off their dirty clothes, and taking a quick bath. On the far side of the tub each fellow was issued clean clothes. I wasn't spying or anything, but I can't believe anyone would take a bath every single day. That is taking cleanliness to an extreme. Though I've got to think that it would be a lot better than working around some of my crew, who smell like they've lived their whole lives in a horse barn.

May 1

The big celebration for joining the rails is scheduled for May 8. All of the company officials from both sides will be here to brag up the occasion. I hope the speeches aren't too long.

I wrote to John and told him that we'll be headed home before the month is out.

May 3

The work has slowed to a snail's pace. More men are being laid off each day, but a lot of them are sticking around to watch the final ceremony. The men say that the railway officials have got two solid gold spikes ready for the occasion. Boy, would I like to take a swing at them.

Durant and a bunch of fancy gents and reporters — as if we need more newspaper people around here — will be traveling by special train to attend the ceremony.

May 6

The celebration has been delayed due to a kidnapping! Some workers back in Piedmont who haven't been paid for months have taken Durant hostage. They've switched his personal car onto a sidetrack and chained the wheels to the rails. According to our telegraph man, they aren't going to let him go until they get every dollar of their back pay — in cash.

It couldn't have happened to a nicer fellow.

May 7

With nothing else for the fellows to do, there's lots of drinking and fighting going on. Two little tent cities called Deadfall and Last Chance have sprung up near here. Twenty men have been killed in the last twenty days.

May 8

Durant finally got money shipped in to pay off the workers in Piedmont, but it didn't do him a lick of good because he's now being held up by his own bad tracks. The bridges are so weak in Echo Canyon that they are hauling in carloads of lumber to make repairs. And the trestle is so bad at Devil's Gate that an engineer is refusing to drive his train over the bridge until it is reinforced.

Pa was sure right to worry about the shoddy track.

May 9
Promontory Summit, Utah (mile 1,086)

The C.P. and U.P. crews are now within a rail's length of each other but we are waiting for the arrival of officials from both companies. The C.P. directors were delayed by a log that fell across the tracks near Truckee, California, and damaged their locomotive. They are sending out another engine to fetch them.

May 10

Last night General Casement pulled a fast one on the C.P. Though the government declared Promontory Summit as the meeting place for the two railroads, they didn't say who had the right to build a station here. So

146

when Casement heard that the C.P. was planning to put in a siding at daybreak, he did them one better.

He got us moving shortly after dark, and we worked through a good part of the night to put the tracks down. When the C.P. work train pulled up at dawn, they found our locomotives and cars parked on a half mile of finished siding. They took it pretty well, and seeing as how they had so recently broken our tracklaying record, I considered it a well-deserved comeuppance.

A few people started gathering for the ceremony early in the morning, but the main crowd didn't form until shortly after lunch. Along with Durant and Leland Stanford, a reverend, a bishop, four governors, and two congressmen were all waiting to take their turn at blessings and speeches. In addition to the two golden spikes there was a silver one from Nevada-Comstock, and a mixed silver, gold, and iron one from the Arizona Territory. A laurel-wood tie was waiting to receive the final spikes, and there was even a fancy silver sledge for the pounding.

When the big moment arrived, two bands struck up a march, and a double-file procession of soldiers aligned themselves along the tracks. U.P. workers set a rail in place on our side as a group of Chinese clad in neat blue smocks and wearing "coolie" hats picked up another rail and stepped toward the open place on their side. Just then Bill Flanagan called out, "Shoot," to a photographer, meaning he should take a picture. The Chinese fellows, who thought "shoot" meant something else, dropped their rail and ran for cover. The fellows in the crowd roared.

As I stood there watching Pa and Bill and the rest of them laugh, I felt sorry for those Chinese fellows. I caught the attention of a young man who had run past me, and waved for him to come back. I picked up his hat and handed it to him. When the Chinese gathered back together, I helped them carry the rail over and set it in place.

As I stepped back, Pa looked at me strange. I couldn't tell whether he was mad or not. Both crews began driving plain iron spikes down the length of the last two rails. They were saving the gold and silver ones for that special laurel tie.

Our fellows had just hammered the last spike down on their side when the Chinese man I'd helped tapped me on the shoulder. He handed me his maul and pointed toward a spike that he'd already started. I shook my head, but he motioned toward the spike again and smiled. I had no choice but to step forward.

When I bent down and tapped the spike to make sure it was firmly set, Mac O'Grady called out, "No cheating," meaning I had to drive it down in just three hits. I looked over at him, ready to scowl, but I was surprised to see him grinning alongside Pa. "He's right, Sean," Pa called, smiling as big as I'd ever seen him smile. "Take it down on your own."

As I balanced the hickory handle in my hands, I remembered Pa's advice about letting the maul do the work, and I also thought back to the Chinese crew I'd watched working last month. I wanted that same easy rhythm.

I lifted my arms and swung smooth. A clear, metallic *ping* rang out over the heads of the crowd. Keeping that tempo, I swung a second time and hit it clean again. Then for the final blow, I did the same, snapping my wrists down hard at the last second. The *clink* told me that I'd buried the spike tight against the rail. The U.P. fellows let out a little cheer, and that Chinese man clapped me on the shoulder as he took his maul back.

Then the officials stepped forward for the final show. Since they didn't want to ding up those gold and silver spikes, Governor Stanford and Durant took turns tapping them into four predrilled holes in the shiny laurelwood tie. Then, as soon as the pictures were taken, some workers slid a regular tie into place and hammered home all the common iron spikes but one.

As a telegraph operator stood ready to signal the final joining of the rails to the rest of the country, Governor Stanford took the first swing. He lifted the spike maul way above his head and pulled down clumsily. He missed by six inches, and his maul clanged on the rail. The boys roared, and this time, I laughed right along.

The governor sheepishly handed the maul to Durant, who pushed up the sleeves of his black velvet coat and took a turn. Durant's swing was even more feeble than Stanford's, and he missed the spike completely, too. As Durant's maul dinged against the rail, the fellows yowled.

Bill Flanagan hollered, "We'da never made it outa Omaha with spiking like that!"

To finish things off, our chief engineer, Sam Reed, and Strobridge stepped in and made quick work of the last spike, saving the final hit for Strobridge's wife, Hannah. When she outdid both Stanford and Durant by nailing the spike with a solid rap, everyone cheered and applauded.

Finally, with men crowded onto every deck and platform, the U.P.'s *Engine 119* and the C.P.'s *Jupiter* nosed together over the newly joined rails. Though the green-and-black *119* was a bit plainer than the *Jupiter*, which had a big balloon-stack chimney and red-spoked drive wheels, every piece of brass on both engines was shining. The engineers, each holding a bottle of champagne, climbed up beside their headlights as the fellows on the ground hooted and hollered over the hiss of steam.

The loudest cheer of all went up when they broke the bottles over the front of each engine, and U.P. engineer Sam Bradford tipped his cap to the crowd. Following the explosion of foam and glass, both engineers shook hands and returned to their cabs. The Jupiter backed up a few hundred yards so *Engine 119* could pull its passengers into C.P. territory. Then the *119* returned the favor.

The only disappointment came when A. J. Russell, the photographer who'd gotten a perfect shot of Durant missing the spike, dropped his glass exposure plate on the ground. It shattered into a million pieces, destroying the picture that would've proved what a puffed-up bunch of incompetents these rich folks are.

May 11

There's something sad about a job—even a tough job like this—being over. It doesn't help that the camp has been so quiet all day. Yesterday, everything was in a constant ruckus. As soon as the ceremony was over, people went crazy for souvenirs. They took jackknives to the "last" tie and cut it up into so many little slivers that we had to replace it three times. I hope they keep a close watch on those golden spikes.

Today, most of the fellows were suffering from too much celebrating, and they lay in bed until way after lunch. The two railroads had made the mistake of footing the bill for an end-of-the-job celebration, and the boys got more carried away than usual.

Pa and I had a long talk tonight while we were walking back from the dining car. I was afraid that seeing this job end might bring back the war memories that used to put him into those long, black silences. But he's been more talkative than ever lately. He said, "Building this railroad was something big, Sean. Not only have we played a part in changing this country forever, but I've had the chance to see my water boy grow into a heck of a spiker."

He went on to talk about how the Northern Pacific was going to build a rail line all the way out to Seattle by way of Montana. "They plan on starting next year," he said. "We might want to think about signing on. Why, we could even ask your brother to come along. That would make us a real family again."

I thought about how excited John would be at the invitation, as Pa stared down the tracks like he was measuring the miles of rail we'd laid. Then, almost in a whisper, he added, "I know your ma woulda liked that."

★ ★ ★

May 12

It's way too quiet around here. I always thought I'd be so happy when this job was done. A month ago, I could picture myself throwing my hat in the air and letting out a big "Yahoo" when we put the last spike down. But now that the day has come and gone, I can't help but feel sad.

One day, I'm working on the top rail crew; then, I wake up the very next morning as a boy without a job. Stopping all this tracklaying so suddenly has given me a hint of what a shock it must have been for Pa when the Civil War ended.

May 19

After the final joining of the rails, Pa and I worked an extra week "mopping up," as he called it. Then we caught a train bound for Chicago.

I just read in the paper that Bill Thompson, the fellow I met in Omaha with his scalp in a bucket when I first came West, has returned to England. According to the story, the Omaha doctor couldn't reattach his hair, but Thompson was so grateful to him for trying that he had his scalp tanned and gave it to him as a present. They say it's still on display in the doctor's window.

It's hard to believe that happened almost two years ago.

Traveling back East, we've seen hundreds of brand-new ties and rails and spikes piled up at nearly every station. Pa figures that Durant got money under the table for all the materials he purchased. So the more he bought, the more he filled his own pockets. Most everything will get used, though, because crews have already started to repair some of the shoddy work that couldn't pass government inspection.

It used to take a half a year to sail the eighteen thousand miles from New York to San Francisco, but these iron ribbons can take a man across this whole country in only a week.

May 20

This morning we passed through Benton, or what's left of it. Though Laramie and Cheyenne have new waves of settlers arriving daily, Benton lasted less than a month. No one ever hit a good well, so the people all picked up and left. Our conductor calls Benton "the shortest-lived city in the history of the West."

Julesburg is as dead as Benton. That's especially strange, since it was one of the liveliest of all the hell-on-wheels towns to spring up along the U.P. line. But Ben once told me that where there's boom, there's bust. I can see how true that is. Except for the piles of old broken bottles, rusting cans, and scraps of lumber, there's nothing left to hint that five thousand people were crowding the streets only a year ago.

Sometimes at night, I lay awake and wonder if they ever caught the man who killed that fellow I found lying with his pockets turned out. I can still see his eyes locked in the middle of an unfinished thought and staring straight up at heaven.

Afternoon

It's true what Pa told me when I first came West. The wildflowers and the prairie grass are a sight to behold. I guarantee that those long weeks working in the Red Desert have given me an appreciation for all things green and alive.

When we were taking on water this afternoon, I saw a man on horseback approaching from the south. The bluestem grass was so tall that his horse disappeared altogether, and it looked like he was floating over a rippling sea.

There is a rare beauty to this land. In an instant the wind can shift the color of the prairie grass from a whitish green to a deep purple and back again. Splashes of wildflowers color everything up, too. And along with the buffalo that have survived the hunters are big herds of antelope; and flocks of prairie chickens, quail, and doves.

May 21

We stopped for the night in North Platte. Other than the busy rail yard and the locomotive shop, the town looked even more quiet than I remembered. The only sign of fresh activity was the cemetery, which had grown considerably in size. The wooden grave markers were still tilted in all directions — Pa was right when he said that the earth settles fast over a fresh-dug grave.

I read the painted epitaph on a marker and had to fight back a smile. The lines, though they were clearly written from the heart, showed a serious lack of schooling:

> *Here lies Jeemes Engles*
> *hoo was kild by the Shy-an injuns*
> *Juli 1800 and 68.*
> *He was a good egg.*

Who knows what brought James Engles out to these plains? Was he looking for work? Hiding from the law? Like so many of the fellows who came West, his life and death will remain a mystery, but that's not to say he didn't count for something.

Ben put it best the day we said good-bye. "Someday you'll probably be riding in a plush car amongst the fancy gents and ladies, Sean, but don't never forget that the backbone of this railroad is the boys that we left buried back along the line."

When I close my eyes, I can see two railroads rushing toward each other and into history, leaving an army of pick-and-shovel men behind. I'll do my best to make sure that the workers who built this line are not forgotten.

I saw a lone bull buffalo today, galloping along the crest of a hill. When the train whistled, he stopped and turned toward us. He lowered his head and pawed the grass, looking ready to charge. Then, all of a sudden, his tail flicked up like a young colt, and he pranced away. Lots of folks say it won't be long before the buffalo are all gone, but I'm hoping they can hang on. Only time will tell.

Epilogue

Sean and Pa returned to Chicago in May of 1869. The following year, they traveled, along with Sean's brother, John, to Fargo, North Dakota, and signed on with a Northern Pacific Railroad construction crew.

Ben Wharton went south to work on the construction of the Atchison, Topeka & Santa Fe Railroad. He later moved to New Orleans and became a conductor for the Southern Pacific Railroad, where he worked until his retirement in 1903.

In 1871 a fire burned down a third of Chicago. Uncle Willy and Aunt Katie lost their home. The factory that employed Uncle Willy also burned down, and he found work with an old neighbor of his named George Pullman, who was building railroad passenger cars.

Once the Northern Pacific Railroad was finished in 1883, the Sullivan men returned to Chicago. Pa hired on with his old railroad, the Chicago and Alton line. He worked as a section-gang foreman until his retirement in 1898. Sean was surprised to hear that Jimmy Flynn had moved to Chicago and started a steak house that had become one of the most popular restaurants in town.

At a double-wedding ceremony in July of 1884, Sean and John married two sisters named Molly and Margaret Branscomb. Both couples moved to Lake Calumet and were neighbors of Uncle Willy and Aunt Katie. Sean and John went to work for the rapidly growing Pullman Palace Car Company.

When the Pullman workers went on strike in 1894, Sean met the famous socialist Eugene Debs. Sean was impressed with Debs's ideas on workers' rights and when he saw the strikebreaking tactics of the Pullman Company, he decided to become a labor activist. Sean went to work for the American Railway Union and spent the rest of his life working in the Chicago area as a union organizer.

John also quit the Pullman Company and went to work for a man named William Wrigley, who had just introduced a new spearmint flavor of chewing gum.

Sean and Molly had three daughters and two sons. Two of their daughters became schoolteachers, and one became a suffragette, who dedicated her life to campaigning for women's right to vote. One of Sean's sons went to work for the McCormick Harvesting Machine Company, which had been founded by Cyrus McCormick, the inventor of the mechanical reaper. The other son became an engineer on the Chicago and North Western Railroad, continuing the family tradition of working on the railroad.

Following their retirements, Sean and John started a guiding service on Lake Michigan. They specialized in walleye fishing and operated their popular charter boat until 1928. Sean died on May 10, 1931, at the age of 79.

Life in America
in 1867

Historical Note

★　★　★

The completion of the transcontinental railroad in May of 1869 is an achievement that is often compared in both scope and difficulty with America's effort to put a man on the moon one hundred years later. This comparison is particularly apt, for the 1969 Apollo space mission concluded a decade that was filled with the same sort of social unrest that pulled our country apart in the 1860s. In the same way that President Kennedy inspired U.S. citizens to rally in support of the space program, Abraham Lincoln urged his fellow Americans, who were then in the midst of a great Civil War, to put their full effort behind the building of a railroad that would connect New York and San Francisco.

When a telegraph operator at the golden spike ceremony clicked out the message signaling the completion of the railroad, wild parties began all across America. Omaha shot off a one-hundred-cannon salute. Chicago hosted a seven-mile-long parade. Philadelphia rang its famous Liberty Bell. Washington, D.C., officials dropped a huge ball from the capitol dome as people cheered, and in every little town throughout the country, factory whistles screeched, fireworks exploded, and crowds roared.

Back in 1856, people had laughed at Theodore Judah when he had suggested that the United States build a railroad from New York to San Francisco. "Crazy Judah," the newspapers called him. They drew cartoons and wrote editorials making fun of him. Yet he refused to give up his dream.

Unlike Dr. Hartwell Carver and John Plumbe, who had petitioned Congress to build a transcontinental railroad in 1832 and 1838, respectively; and unlike Asa Whitney, who had proposed building a railroad from Lake Michigan to the Pacific Ocean in 1848, Judah refused to give up. He was so committed to his idea that he continually lobbied Congress from 1856 to 1859 to authorize the construction of the transcontinental railroad.

Judah knew that with the discovery of gold in California and the rapid growth that had followed, America needed to link its east and west coasts with an efficient system of transportation. Traveling to California by ship took from six to nine months depending on the weather, and shipwrecks were a fact of life that travelers had to accept. Overland travel by wagon was equally dangerous. The trip took several months, and the risks of being killed by bandits or Indians, or dying from exposure during the desert and mountain crossings were great.

When Congress ignored Judah's petitions, he went West at his own expense and surveyed a rail line through the rugged Sierra Nevada Mountains. As an experienced engineer, Judah plotted a workable route and estimated the miles of track and the length of the many tunnels that would be needed to cross the mountains. Despite the fact that his survey proved the railroad could be built, Congress refused to act.

The main problem stalling Congress was the slavery issue. The South feared that if the West was opened up to settlement, the new states would join the antislavery coalition of the North. They couldn't risk upsetting the balance of power. Steamship and stagecoach companies also lobbied hard against the railroad, knowing that they would lose much of their business.

Though most people still insisted on calling Theodore Judah by his nickname, "Crazy Judah," four wealthy California businessmen finally listened. In 1860 Collis Huntington, Mark Hopkins, Charles Crocker, and Leland Stanford met with Judah and offered him financial support. A year later these men, who soon became known as "the Big Four," organized the Central Pacific Railroad Company. At this same time the Civil War began, and with the secession of the South, opposition to the transcontinental railroad suddenly disappeared.

At the urging of President Abraham Lincoln, Congress

quickly passed the Pacific Railroad Act of 1862. The terms of this act were generous, offering mileage payments that varied according to the difficulty of the terrain. The government backed flatlands at $16,000 per mile; the foothills $32,000; and the mountains $48,000. The Railroad Act also granted huge tracts of land for every mile of track completed. Not only were the railroad companies offered a two-hundred-foot right-of-way on either side of their tracks, they were also given alternate sections of land that totaled 6,400 acres per mile.

"The Big Four" immediately began scheming to see how they could make more money. They set up a corporation called the Contract and Finance Company and hired themselves to do $32 million worth of work for a fee of $90 million. They also planned to overcharge the government by lying about where the mountains really began, thereby increasing their mileage payments.

When Judah found out that his partners were dishonest, he immediately set sail for New York, hoping to replace his investors with men who were more interested in the public good. However, while taking a shortcut across Panama, Judah contracted yellow fever and died shortly after. He would never see his dream become a reality.

The Union Pacific followed the same pattern of

dishonesty and public deception. Thomas Durant, one of the founders of the Union Pacific, got together with a speculator named George Train, and started a company called the Credit Mobilier of America. Like the C.P.'s Contract and Finance Company, the U.P.'s Credit Mobilier was set up for the sole purpose of overcharging the government and the U.P.'s stockholders. If the actual cost of construction was $30,000 per mile, the U.P. typically charged $50,000.

Because both Durant and the "Big Four" were making huge contributions to congressional campaigns—Collis Huntington alone gave five hundred thousand dollars a year to congressmen—the government was slow to look into the conduct of the railroads. The U.P. even tried to hold off investigations by selling company stock to congressmen at a big discount.

By the time Congress finally got around to checking the records, the railroad builders had literally taken their money and run. Estimates vary over the amount of cash that these officials swindled from the government. An 1873 New York *Sun* newspaper article that examined the building of the transcontinental railroad claimed that the C.P. directors had pocketed at least $63 million during their construction project. Further investigation revealed that the U.P. had billed the government $73 million for only $50 million of work.

However, charges were never filed against any of these men. Huntington avoided prosecution by claiming that a fire had destroyed all his records; Durant retired to the Catskill Mountains and remained silent during the investigations; Stanford went on to endow the university that bears his name and later accepted an appointment to the U.S. Senate; while Crocker built a $1,250,000 mansion. The only official from either company who did his best to tell the truth was Oakes Ames of the U.P. For his honesty, he was condemned by a vote of congressional censure, while his associates escaped blame. The well-intentioned Ames was humiliated and he died shortly thereafter.

As sad a comment as this makes on the life of Oakes Ames and the thousands of other honest Americans who were swindled out of their money, the objective of the Railroad Act was accomplished. While only five miles of railroads existed in this country in 1852, by 1890 there were 72,000 miles of track. Railways quickly became the lifeline of American commerce. Industrial products, raw materials, and people could move with an ease that had previously been unimaginable.

By linking our two coasts together, the transcontinental railroad brought instant prosperity to the Great Plains. As additional rail lines were built, rising real estate values attracted waves of land developers and speculators from back East. The market demand also increased for lumber and for silver, lead, and copper ores that were shipped back East for processing and sale to rapidly expanding industries. Farmers could now market their crops efficiently, and factories could supply the settlers with manufactured goods. With access to new plows and harvesting equipment, advanced strains of seeds, and superior breeds of livestock, farm production soared. And as the farmer's productivity increased, so did the East's demand for their products, fueling an agricultural boom that transformed the West from an open wilderness to a series of rail-connected settlements in only a few short decades.

Though the building of the transcontinental railroad represented a great accomplishment, there was also a darker side to this achievement: In their haste to complete their project, the railroad barons did much harm that could have been avoided. They swindled investors out of hard-earned money. They took advantage of thousands of immigrant workers, reducing the Chinese in particular to the status of slave labor. They also encouraged the killing of great herds of buffalo and the confinement of large numbers of Native American people to marginal lands called reservations. At its best, this new railroad proved the theory of Manifest Destiny — the concept that it was our God-given right to claim all the land west of the Mississippi—but at its worst, it represented unbridled greed.

The trip from New York to San Francisco, which had taken as long as eight or nine months by ship before the coming of the railroad, could now be accomplished in a single week. Theodore Judah's dream of linking our shores had finally been realized. Though Judah had died several years before the golden spike ceremony, when Governor Stanford commissioned an artist to paint the famous event, he made a special request that Judah be pictured alongside the honored joiners of the rails. So in death the visionary Judah ironically took his rightful place beside the founders of the transcontinental railroad.

After grading the roadbed (top), the workers laid the rails (bottom). The material for one mile of track filled forty railroad cars. Each mile of track took four hundred sections of rail (weighing almost six hundred pounds each), twenty-four hundred wooden ties, and four thousand iron spikes.

In the great race to build the transcontinental railroad, Thomas Clark Durant led the Union Pacific Railroad Company. Durant's obsession with wealth was evident in his flamboyant suits and coats and his penchant for hosting lavish parties. He hoped that gaining control of the Union Pacific would allow him to make lots of money quickly, and he cofounded the Credit Mobilier for just that purpose.

172

Theodore Dehone Judah was an American railroad engineer who played an important role in laying the groundwork for the transcontinental railroad. He worked tirelessly to gather both political and financial support for the venture. With the financial backing of four prominent railroad investors, known as the "Big Four," Judah founded the Central Pacific Railroad Company in 1861.

Construction boss General Jack Casement stands proudly in front of his work train, which carried supplies and housed carpenters' and blacksmiths' shops, mess halls, and washhouses. Casement, a fierce-looking former brigadier general, was notorious for the bullwhip he carried.

Railroad workers lived in dormitory cars like these (top), which were part of Casement's construction train. Because the sleeping areas smelled horrible and were full of vermin, many workers built and lived in sod huts, like the ones at this graders' camp in Casper, Wyoming (bottom).

The Dale Creek Bridge was one of many bridges and tracks laid in haste during the great race. Rails laid on frozen ground buckled during the spring thaw, and some bridges were so weak they could hardly bear a train's weight and were swept away in the spring floods. All of this unusable track eventually had to be relaid, at enormous costs.

Benton, Wyoming, was one of many "hell-on-wheels" towns, which were known for their rough-and-tumble saloons and dance halls. These towns provided workers with little to spend their money on but liquor, gambling, and women, often resulting in drunken brawls, shootings, and knifings. Two months after Benton was set up, it was deserted, with only trash, abandoned shacks, and a cemetery full of murder victims left behind.

In the Fort Laramie treaty of 1868, the land west of the Missouri River was promised as a permanent home for the Plains Indians, including Sioux, Lakota, Arapaho, Cheyenne, and other tribes. Angered when the railroad moved across the Missouri River and into their hunting grounds, the Indians began to attack the railroad workers (top) and the railroad itself, uprooting rails and tearing down telegraph wires. The railroad, and the settlers that would follow it, threatened the Plains Indians' land and buffalo (bottom), which they depended on for their material and spiritual value.

Although the Central Pacific Railroad workers had frequent delays on their eastward-moving path because of snow in the High Sierra, once the Union Pacific Railroad got as far west as the Rocky Mountains, they, too, had trouble with drifting snow covering the tracks. Here, Union Pacific workers begin the difficult task of shoveling out a snowbound train.

Many of the Irish, German, and Italian immigrants employed by the Union Pacific believed themselves to be far superior to the Central Pacific's Chinese workers. The difference in their wages served to reinforce this discrimination: The Chinese earned between $27 and $30 a month, while other immigrant workers were earning $35 a month. As the rails neared Promontory Summit, the crews were working side by side. Tensions rose, and workers on both sides were killed as a result of explosions that were deliberately set off without warning.

The No. 1 General Sherman was built by Danforth, Cooke & Company of Paterson, New Jersey, and was brought by steamboat to Omaha, Nebraska, in June 1865. This woodburning engine was the top of the line of all motive power used by the Union Pacific Railroad.

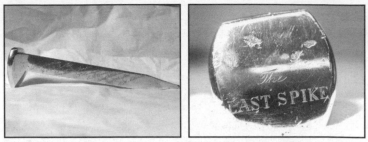

The "golden spike" that was to join the two sides of the railroad on May 10, 1869, was not golden at all: The gold and silver spikes that were initially dropped into place were discreetly removed and replaced with ordinary iron spikes. Embarrassingly, both Leland Stanford of the Central Pacific and Thomas Durant of the Union Pacific missed the spike when they took their swings. In the end, it was a regular rail worker—one who had probably driven thousands of spikes in his work on the railroad—who drove the last spike and ended the race.

After the last spike was driven at Promontory Summit, Utah, the Jupiter of the Central Pacific (left) and the No. 119 of the Union Pacific (right) were moved nose-to-nose. The engineers broke champagne bottles on each other's trains, and a telegraph operator gave the three-dot signal for "done," initiating celebrations across the country.

This broadsheet advertises the grand opening of the transcontinental railroad.
With the completion of the railroad, settlers poured into the West. Able to go
cross-country in six or seven days, they no longer had to face a month-long trip
by rail and stagecoach or an arduous five-month-long journey by wagon train.

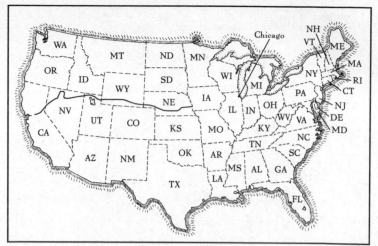

Modern map of the contintental United States, showing Chicago, Illinois, and the transcontinental railroad.

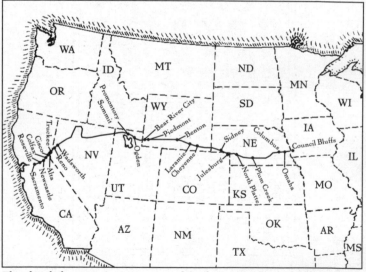

This detail shows important stations along the transcontinental railroad route, along with Promontory Summit, Utah, where the two sides of the railroad were joined.

About the Author

★ ★ ★

William Durbin is the author of many critically acclaimed novels for young readers, including *The Broken Blade, Wintering, The Darkest Evening, El Lector,* and *The Winter War,* among others. His works have garnered honors such as Junior Library Guild Selection, Bank Street College Children's Book of Year list, American Library Association's Amelia Bloomer list, New York Library Books for the Teen Age list, Great Lakes Book Award, Minnesota Book Award, Maud Hart Lovelace nomination, Jefferson Cup Series of Note Award, America's Award commended title, and a Book Sense Summer Pick.

William Durbin says, "I was inspired to try my hand at writing for young people after I met a fellow Minnesotan named Gary Paulsen at a writing conference. Though I'd mainly been publishing poetry and critical essays, he convinced me that writing for kids was more rewarding. 'Write what's real,' he said, 'and kids will respond.' I've been trying to follow his advice ever since."

A former teacher, William Durbin has supervised writing research projects for the National Council of Teachers of English and Middlebury College's Bread

Loaf School of English. He lives on Lake Vermilion in Northeastern Minnesota with his wife, Barbara. They have a son, Reid, and a daughter, Jessica.

For additional information, visit his website at williamdurbin.com.

Acknowledgments

★ ★ ★

I would like to extend special thanks to my editor, Amy Griffin, and to the production staff at Scholastic for the care they have taken in the preparation of this manuscript.

For assistance with my research I would like to recognize Bob Hanover of the Golden Spike Monument; Lori Olson of the American Heritage Center at the University of Wyoming; Thomas Taber of the Railroad Historical Research Center; Don Snoddy of the Union Pacific Railroad Museum in Omaha; and the staffs of the Wilson Library at the University of Minnesota, the University of Minnesota Duluth Library, and the Virginia Public Library.

Finally, my gratitude, as always, must go to my wife, Barbara; my daughter, Jessica; and my son, Reid, for their unflagging support.

★ ★ ★

Page 171 (bottom): Railroad building on the Great Plains, Library of Congress.

Page 172: Thomas Clark Durant, Union Pacific Railroad Museum.

Page 173: Theodore Judah, ibid.

Page 174: General Jack Casement with work train, ibid.

Page 175 (top): Dormitory cars, Great Northern Railway Historical Society Archives.

Page 175 (bottom): Graders' camp, Union Pacific Railroad Museum.

Page 176 (top): Dale Creek Bridge, *The American West in the Nineteenth Century*, Dover Publications, Inc., Mineola, New York.

Page 176 (bottom): Benton, Wyoming, Union Pacific Railroad Museum.

Page 177 (top): Confrontation between Plains Indians and railroad workers, *The American West in the Nineteenth Century*, Dover Publications, Inc., Mineola, New York.

Page 177 (bottom): Train surrounded by buffalo, *Ready-to-Use Old West Cuts*, Dover Publications, Inc., Mineola, New York.

Page 178: Snowbound train, North Wind Picture Archives.

Page 179 (top): Explosion near railroad workers, *The American West in the Nineteenth Century*, Dover Publications, Inc., Mineola, New York.

Page 179 (bottom): The *No. 1 General Sherman* engine, Hulton Archive/Getty Images.

Page 180 (top, left and right): The Last Spike, gold alloyed with copper, William T. Garrett Foundry, San Francisco, 1869, gift of David Hewes to Stanford University, Iris & B. Gerald Cantor Center for Visual Arts.

Page 180 (bottom): The joining of the rails, Union Pacific Railroad Museum.

Page 181: Broadsheet, ibid.

Page 182: Maps by Heather Saunders.